The Carter Cartel: Lynx Carter

K. RENEE

CHAPTER 1

Brayden Lynx Carter

It was a little after three in the morning, and I was supposed to be home in bed with my beautiful wife. Instead, I'm walking into a dingy ass warehouse ready to murk a nigga or two. Fuck! These muthafuckas are always trying to get the upper hand on the next nigga instead of staying in the lane that was paved for their ass, but nooo! These muthafuckas gotta come into my shit and think we're just going to let them sit and have a good muthafuckin' time! Especially these Mexican and Puerto Rican niggas.

The musty smell of the rustic walls was enough to make a nigga dizzy. Looking around, I made a mental note to have somebody give this bitch a facelift. Right now, though, I was focusing on the task at hand so that I could go home and get my dick wet.

"Noooo! Fuck! Arghhhhh! Lynx, please! I had nothing to

do with it, please. I'll give you eighty percent of my earnings if you let me live! Please spare me! I have a family to care for! Please!"

I took a seat in the chair that was sitting in front of pussy ass Masio Lopez while his cries fell on deaf ears. Mel passed me a lit cigar and a glass of Deleon while I leaned back in my seat and contemplated on how I was going to kill this fat fuck. Because despite his pleas, you better believe his bitch ass is gonna die. My hesitation stemmed from me trying to figure out an approach. Sometimes, I like to switch shit up.

"Money means a lot to me, but it's not everything. It damn sure doesn't mean shit, when it comes to my family and friends, I consider family. You killed my best friend, one of the most loyal people in my camp. You went in his house and violated his wife and her mother in the worst way. You killed them. Then you killed their beautiful daughter and son, and you think I'm going to let you and these pussy ass niggas walk out of here alive?"

Just thinking about the five white and gold caskets -two of them being half the size of the other three - caused a pain in my chest. Anger almost choked me as I sipped the glass of premium tequila. Now wasn't the time to breakdown though. I had to show only one emotion – *Hatred*.

"One thing I've always stood by is that you deal with the street nigga you're gunning for, but you leave their families alone UNLESS they come for your family. Then all bets are off. I'm killing every fuckin' body about mine. You foreigner muthafuckas don't know shit about morals! You a pussy muthafucka, Lopez, and these bitch niggas hanging beside you are pussy too! Just know the moment I kill you niggas, it's lights out for your bitches too.

I won't go low though. Nah, I'm too real to go as low as you did. I won't touch your children, but they will grow up with nothing, and I do mean nothing. Mack was my nigga a hundred grand, and since he can't get his revenge, I'ma step in and get that shit for him!" I spoke calmly, but firm enough for these muthafuckas to know it was lights out in a gruesome fuckin' way!

Mack came from New York with me when I took over this organization. He was a hardcore man who worked his ass off for me. He was loyal as fuck, and that was my best friend and brother. Just because we didn't have the same blood running through our veins didn't mean shit. Lopez and his crew caught my nigga slippin', ran up in his house, and took him and his family out. That shit damn near killed me because my friend didn't deserve that shit.

We also live by the code of the streets. It's a saying they have, you live by the sword, and you die by that muthafucka. Well, that saying has shown up in this warehouse tonight. When I stood to my feet, my cousin Nori took the machete he was holding and began slashing these niggas one by one in their chests and stomachs. Guts and taco juice spewed from their abdomens, making me nod my head in approval. One thing about Nori is that nigga was hard as fuck when it came to this game. He didn't spare shit with these muthafuckas. He didn't give a fuck about your cries or pleas for your life. If it's in his mind that you're going to die, the only thing he's thinking about is how you will die.

Malik lowered the chains, and Mel started dashing acid on their wounds. Their screams of agony were music to my ears. Their suffering was imperative, and it was only fair I inflicted the same pain they did on my boy. The home security system Mack had, allowed us to watch the shit play out, and these muthafuckas were gruesome with it. I had to pause it numerous times to gather myself before I got to the end. Shit was fucked up in so many ways. They made him watch them violate his wife, and her mother, then kill them and his kids. So, yeah, it's up and showtime in this bitch. My phone beeped, letting me know I had a text message.

> Wifey: So, I guess this is another
> later night? Do better, Lynx!

Drowning out weakened cries, I sighed because I hated letting her down. Sometimes balancing work and home was challenging as fuck. Before my wife and son, I didn't have to worry about checking in or respecting hours. Now that I had a family, I tried my best to uphold the image of a normal husband, but the reality is I'm far from normal. As a matter of fact, I'm the furthest thing from normal. I'm Lynx mutha-fuckin' Carter! Head of the Carter Cartel. But to my wife, I was her man, her rib, the head of household, and tonight I was letting her down once again.

I didn't even bother responding to her message because I felt like I was repeating myself when I explained that I'm trying, but this is a part of the business. Putting my phone away, I gave my attention to these fucks in front of me, snapping back in action.

"Bring them in!" I ordered. The door opened, and Mel pulled the wives, girlfriends, and mothers of these niggas in the room. The moment they saw them, these niggas were kicking and screaming, damn near ripping their arms from the chains trying to get down and save their loved ones. To spice some shit up, I threw in their side chicks too. They must've all known about each other because instead of being mad that they were about to die, they were side-eying and mugging each other, even though they were duct taped and chained. The mothers, however, were either crying real tears or just staring blankly at the fuck ups they call sons.

Oh, when I said I'm killing them bitches, I meant tonight! My wife was already tripping, so there was no way in hell I was putting this off another night and risking not getting any pussy, or her not speaking to me for a week. I decided to make this shit quick.

Pulling both of my guns from my waist, I sent multiple shots in their heads, dropping them one by one. One of the chicks was a real one. She at least tried to fight for her life. Didn't end in her favor, but I respect her will to live.

Nori whistled, "Them was some bad ass bitches too. Damn."

"Argghhhhh! You pussy nigga! Oh my God, mi Madre! Noooooooooo!" Lopez screamed and tried his best to kick at me through his pain. Placing my guns back in my waist, I lifted the machete and severed that nigga's head. That shit hit the concrete with a splat and rolled near Malik's feet. His crazy ass jumped back like it was infected or something.

Nori took care of the rest of dumb ass crew while I went to shower before going home to my wife. It was no way I was going in the house with the stench of musk and death. Plus, I wanted to be able to go in the house and curl up next to my wife the moment I crossed the threshold. I was tired as fuck and ready to get some sleep. An hour later, after washing my ass and standing underneath the water longer than I intended, I walked back to the lower level of the warehouse. Even though the bottom level could use some work due to all the acid we used that ate away the walls and floors, my upstairs was immaculate and could easily be lived in.

"His territory is now up for grabs. Give it to the highest bidder, and our percentages of the money earned goes to Mack's mom and sister. When does our shipment come in?" I asked, looking over at Malik.

"In a few days," he answered.

"Make sure all the heads are here for a round table meeting. If these muthafuckas decide they want to try us, they will get the same fuckin' treatment Lopez got. If a muthafucka feel like they want to poke they chest out, I'll pull his bitch ass heart out at the table and feed that shit to my Pits. The percentages that are due to us are going up; I'm not playing with them. They want a seat at my table; they gotta pay to get in the muthafuckin room," I explained.

I think watching my wife push out my son caused me to go

fucking soft for the last few years, and that's why muthafuckas like Lopez thought it was safe to try us. Well, that shit was over with now. I was back on my bully shit!

"It's whatever you wanna do. They gon' be down with us or choose to go to war with us. Either way, it's up." Malik shrugged and headed for the door. I spoke with Mel and Nori for a few more minutes before finally heading home. I felt as if that weight was lifted off me, because now my boy could rest. I couldn't rest until we got the muthafuckas that did that shit to them. I'm glad Nori and Mel were on the next flight immediately to assist in handling this because this shit was personal for all of us. I knew I would have to hear my wife's mouth about my late nights, but that's nothing new. I just need to figure out how to adjust my time to be there for her.

CHAPTER 2

Lynx

Six Months Later

If a muthafucka would have told me I would turn into a wholesome ass family man, I would have called them a liar. My heart is smiling inside as I lay here watching my wife move around the bedroom as she gets ready for her lunch date with Bria. I love everything about my woman. From the way she sways her fine ass back and forth to the way she loves our child. I love her smell when she steps out of the shower and her intelligence, to the way her glasses sit on the tip of her pointy nose. I love her smart-ass mouth. I love when she pulls her coily, coconut-smelling hair into a messy bun or when she's lying in bed eating junk food, getting crumbs every fucking where. I love her smile, the way she laughs, and even the little snoring she does when she's asleep. Everything about Malayah Carter has my ass smitten.

Marrying her was the best decision I've ever made in my life. If it wasn't enough for me to give that woman my last name, I went and planted a baby in her, making my life even more complete. My wife and son are my reasons, and if my reason is ever tampered with, compromised, or fucked with in any way, that will be the cause of nigga taking their last breath. There can never be an explanation regarding why someone fucked with my family, EVER! You fuck with them, you die! It's just that simple. Some will say *nigga, you pussy whipped*, and I'd definitely have to agree it's all of the above for me. I'll never be ashamed to admit this love is like nothing I've ever experienced before.

In these streets, I'm a muthafuckin' boss, head of the deadliest Cartel on this side of the globe. Who will slice your throat and walk away without a care in the world, but when it comes to my wife, I'm just a man in love.

"Braydennn!" Malayah's voice came flowing through the intercom, and I had to chuckle because she knew I hated her singing my legal shit like that. Plus, her ass was only in the bathroom that's connected to our bedroom. She is literally just a few feet away from me. Crawling out of bed, I headed inside the bathroom and rested my body against the doorframe.

"Sup, beautiful." My voice was still raspy because I was tired as fuck. I came in late last night, and now my ass was paying for that shit.

Layah turned in my direction, and the biggest smile crept across her face.

"If you were home in bed with your wife last night, you wouldn't be so tired right now. This song and dance about you making time at home is getting old. But I'ma let you live though, lil baby." She smiled, and I had to chuckle at her lil' wannabe hard ass.

"Chill, beautiful. Remember, it's got to be in you, not on you." I winked at her as I moved to handle my hygiene.

Malayah is still as beautiful as the day I first laid eyes on her. Her wild hair had grown even fuller, and birthing my child and taking elite dick every night had her hips spreading every which way. Her soft brown skin glowed as if she was kissed by the sun, and the way her ass was playing peek-a-boo underneath her silk robe had me adjusting my mans in my pajama pants. My wife is truly that one on some real shit.

"Whatever! It's in me. You know who my dad is?" She looked over at me like she really wanted me to answer that shit, but a chortle escaped my lips.

"I know exactly who your dad is, baby. He's the same man that calls me daily to ask if I'm still rich because he doesn't want your money hungry, begging, with a demon seed cartel thugged-out kid coming home and leaching off him with the lil' bit of money he got." We both burst into laughter because my father-in-law is a damn fool. And as time goes by, he only gets worse. One thing I will say about him is that man is as solid they come, and I'll go to war for him any day.

"He really does call you every day."

Malayah spilled some of her curly hair cream into her hands and began working it through her coily strands.

"My dad is nuts. You know he be sending me pictures of other rich Cartel bosses just in case you don't love me no more and kick me out?" Hearing her say that reminded me to call that nigga and tell his ass to stop sending nigga pics to my damn wife. No matter what, I'm not going nowhere, and it isn't shit another Cartel boss can do for my baby. I am THEE Cartel Boss. Can't no nigga compare to Lynx Carter. Them other niggas wouldn't even know what to do with my wife.

"Babe, I want to take a family trip. Can you please make some time in your schedule in the next few months?" She wrapped her arms around my waist, leaning in for a kiss. My wife could be random as hell sometimes, but I always let her rock. If she wants the world, I would easily make that shit happen for her.

"I'm ready whenever you are. Just set the date and let me know." I was still holding her in my arms, and having my wife close always had me ready to serve her ass with these inches. Gripping her ass, I pulled her closer to me, and her ass pulled away quick as hell.

"Nope. Not right now, babe. I'm dressed, and I don't have time to shower and redress. I promised Bri I would be there by one thirty and I have twenty-five minutes to get there. Let's have a date night tonight. We haven't had one in a couple of weeks." She looked up at me, and there was no way that I could ever deny her.

"We can definitely have that." After kissing her lips once

11

more, I turned to step into the shower. A couple of hours later, I was downstairs in the kitchen having lunch and on FaceTime with my cousin Nori.

"How are things going in New York?" I asked Nori.

"So far, everything is good. I'm still looking into that issue with Tez." Hearing him mention that nigga had my trigger finger jumping. A disloyal nigga took me from zero to a hundred quick!

"You know what it is with that. I don't give second chances. He has one time, and if that nigga shows you what it really is, send flowers to his mama and put that nigga to sleep." These niggas knew not to fuck with me, but it's always one that will try you. That's a grave mistake on his part.

"Understood. When are you planning on coming back to New York?"

"Next week, Malayah wants to see her family. What's up? Do you need me to come sooner?" He looked off, and that shit didn't sit right with me. My cousin was like my brother, and I could always tell when some shit was fucking with him.

"Nah, I'm good. Havi has been loyal to us for a long ass time, and I trust what he says. Until I find out that it's something different I'ma rock with him on what he has to say. Let me go handle this shit. It's best I cut that nigga's air supply today! The longer we allow this big muthafucka to be disloyal sends a message to other organizations that it's sweet over here. And ain't a muthafuckin' thing sweet about a nigga like me. That shit irritates the fuck outta me, especially when we've been fair to these muthafuckas."

"I feel you. Send those flowers then, my boy! I'll see you soon." I ended the call with him and shot Malik a quick text.

> Me: We need to head to New York in the next few days. Something seems off with Nori, and we need to make sure he's good. Family first!

> Lik: 'Til the casket drop!

Just as I sat my phone down, it started ringing, and I had to chuckle because it was my crazy ass father in-law. That nigga definitely is one of my favorite people, which is why his ass can say anything to me and get away with it. I knew he was calling to start his shit for the day.

"Sup, Pop!"

"Nigga, what the hell I tell you 'bout that Pop shit? It's bad enough them folks know you married to my daughter. I'm telling you now, if the federales come 'round here asking me questions 'bout your cartel-ish ass, I'ma stick beside you for as long as I can. But the minute them niggas say it's you, or him and his lil' Cartel, thugged out, lil' cockeyed ass baby, you niggas is good as told on. And that's on Mary, her lamb, Jesus Devonte Tupac Shakur Christ, and Mother Afeni." Who the hell was Mother Afeni? Then I had to remember that's was Tupac's mama.

This nigga was unbelievable, and I couldn't stop laughing to even be serious with his ass for a moment. And to top it off, this nigga had a straight ass face. He was serious as hell.

"Bruh, I done told yo' ass to leave my damn child alone!

And my seed ain't damn cockeyed! Where the hell did you even get that from?" I looked at him.

"Seed? You shol' right about that! The lil' nigga is a damn demon seed sprouted from the pits of hell! You may not be able to see it, but I can tell a cockeyed nigga when I see one, and that nigga is on the verge of being cockeyed!" He shrugged.

"That's your grandson. What the hell is wrong with you?!"

"And that thang you married is my daughter, and I ain't let up on her ass yet. She's evil, and I thought I would give her a chance and love her as my daughter the right way, but that shit ain't no fun. Just don't send her ass back here when you decide you don't want her no mo'. I know how you Cartel niggas operate! One minute you in love, and the next minute, you done cut they head off just because her ass looked at Johnny the pool boy for too damn long.

See, I'ma regular drug dealer; we kill differently. Ion got time to be taking niggas body parts and sending them to they mama. That lady could be having a really bad day, and here yo' Pablo Escobar ass come sending her, her son's arm, and his pinky toe. Now she out here trying to protect herself from the Rona virus and yo' ass!

Anyway, I was just calling to see if you still had enough money to take care of my daughter 'cause I hate to see her go from riches to rags." He sat back in his chair with this serious look on his face.

"I can promise you, your daughter will never in her life need a dime of your money. If she chooses to retire right now, she can, and it would still be enough money for her, her children,

THE CARTER CARTEL: LYNX CARTER

their children, and their children. She'll be able to take care of her parents for the rest of their lives. I've created generational wealth for my wife and our offspring. Trust me, you did good, but I got it from here. Oh yeah, stop sending my wife them damn pictures. Can't no nigga take my place or be me," I told him.

"Nigga, you ain't all that. Now, bye!" The phone went black, and I had to look at the shit sideways because this dude really hung up on me. I couldn't help but laugh. That guy was hilarious, and he missed his calling as a comedian. He would've definitely killed the game. I never took anything he said to heart because I knew deep down he was missing the fuck out of his daughter and grandson. I knew it was hard for them, with us living in Puerto Rico, but my baby quickly adjusted to the island life.

"Mr. Carter, you have a phone call on your private line." My house manager's voice came through the intercom.

"Maria, I'm taking my wife out for dinner tonight. You can leave early if you'd like," I announced as I stood from my seat.

"Ok, thank you so much, Mr. Carter." She smiled excitedly. Maria has been with me ever since I moved into this house, but she never takes time off unless I give it to her. There are days that I just say I don't need her so that she can take some time to rest. One thing my aunt did for us was teach us how to cook, and we were damn good at it. She said she never wanted us living on our own and not being able to prepare a meal for ourselves. Walking into my office, I sat at my desk and answered the call on hold.

"Yeah," I spoke into the phone.

"You didn't advise us that you were changing the name of Sandentina's operation!" Hector shouted.

I'm sick of this nigga!

"The fuck is wrong with you?! Who you think you talking too and why the fuck would I let you know that I've changed the name of my damn organization. Sandentina left the shit to me with no stipulations. He didn't leave your ass to watch over me. Let's get this shit clear right now. You were his right hand, not mine. Take that retirement money he left you and retire peacefully. I'm Lynx Carter, and this is my shit, so the Carter Cartel is what it will be." I hung up on his ass, 'cause he got me fucked up.

Hector has always been a little jealous of the relationship I had with Sandentina. He's been dead for years, and the nigga is still keeping tabs on my ass. It's best that he takes my advice and retire because his next move regarding me will be his last move. My ringing phone jolted me out of my thoughts, and I smiled because it was as if she always knew when I needed her to calm me down.

"Hey, Ma. Is everything alright?" I questioned the moment I answered the call.

"Hey, baby. Everything is fine. I just wanted to call and check on you. I haven't heard from you in a couple of weeks, and that's not like you." She was right; it wasn't like me at all when it came down to her. I've always made it my business to call her a few times a week. My aunt was truly my second mom, which is why Malik and I greet her as such, and I loved her with everything in me. She's pulled me out of some really dark places, and I'm forever grateful to her. When my mom died, I thought that was it for me. That shit damn near killed me.

"I'm good, Ma, and I'm sorry for not checking in on you. How are you?" I asked.

"I'm fine. I've been hanging out at the clubhouse and meeting some of my neighbors. I've been here for three years and only know the people next door to me. I'm glad that's changing because I met a new friend, Janice. We've been out to lunch and shopping a few times. She's nice, and I like having a friend close by to do things with."

I was thrilled that she was adapting to the suburban life now. It was hard as hell to get her to leave the hood, but she loved her big house and was forever changing some furniture around and painting a room. Even though we hired the best to do the decorating, she was still switching shit up. I chopped it up to her being bored, so I was glad to hear she'd made a friend.

"Listen, I need you to check on your cousin. I think he broke up with Tasha. I heard him yelling at her, saying it was over. I'm not sure what happened, but make sure he's alright. I've tried to talk to him, but he just brushed it off and wouldn't talk to me about it. I'm worried about him, so check on him for me. It's been a while since I've seen you and Malik. You need to come see me or I'm coming to see you," she stated.

"I'll be there soon." Hearing her say that about Nori reminded me of my call with him earlier. Now I know why things with him seemed off. Shit with him and Tasha ran deep. The two of them were inseparable, and it made sense since they've been together since high school. So, whatever it is with them, the shit must be really bad 'cause Nori is never disrespectful to her from what I've seen. Now what goes on in their home is different because I'm not there, but if my brother needs us, we're there.

"Ok, son. I have some things to take care of before it gets too late. I'll talk to you soon."

"Alright, Ma. Love you."

"Love you too, son." We ended our call, and I shot Malik a message letting him know what's up, and that we were for sure heading to New York in a couple of days. One thing about Nori is he's quiet, but that nigga is a silent assassin. He doesn't do too much talking; he will straight kill yo' ass before you could utter another fuckin' word. He's like me in so many ways. He's a thinker, and that's what makes him the deadliest. His moves are always calculated and precise.

So, once he reflects on any situation and makes a decision, he stands on that shit. Which is why he runs my organization on the US side, and Malik and I handle everything internationally. Now that I think about it, we should probably head to NY tomorrow. This shit with Tasha could go many ways depending on the severity of it. Nori's ass can also, at times, become unhinged.

"Mr. Carter, I've prepared a small spaghetti dinner for Little Bray," Maria informed me as I walked back into the kitchen to grab a bottle of water.

"You didn't have to do that. But I truly appreciate you, Maria."

"I just didn't want you all to have to worry about cooking dinner for him." She smiled, patting me on my back.

"Enjoy the rest of your day off, and take tomorrow off as well. We can handle things around here," I told her.

Maria keeps our home up and running and in top-tier shape. Managing a mansion with a full staff can be a lot, I'd imagine, so I never wanted her to be so enthralled with work and my family that she didn't have time for hers. This wasn't a fucking sweatshop. Besides, with just my wife and son, we were only in our bedrooms, family room, and the kitchen most of the time.

I had to brief my head of security about my outing later with my wife and after that, I decided to hang out with my son for the rest of the day. It's not often that I get to sit around and chill at home, so when time permits, that's all I want to do. With Bray being an only child, I never wanted him to feel lonely. Even though our home was equipped with any and everything a child could want, including an arcade, bowling alley, movie theatre, and indoor and outdoor pool. I built this house with one day having a family in mind, and it's everything I've envisioned it to be. I was going to enjoy this quiet time with my boy, but something in me told me shit was about to get real loud real soon. I just hoped that all it was with Nori was some relationship drama.

CHAPTER 3
Malayah

Bria and I were walking out of the mall to my awaiting truck with my security detail, and the shit she just told me had my head spinning.

I whipped my head in her direction, clutching my imaginary pearls. "Bri, what are you thinking about? If he ever finds out, he's going to be so hurt and pissed!" She was my best friend, and best friends shared their secrets, but damn, I wished she would've kept that shit to herself. She was fighting an internal battle, and I felt so bad for her. I prayed for her strength daily. The day of Bria's baby shower should've been one of the happiest days of their lives. They were having a baby, and Malik had just proposed to her. Their happy moment turned bad quickly, and they literally have been fighting daily for their sanity. When they left our house, Bri wanted ice cream, and without a second thought, Malik took her to get what she wanted.

During the ride, they were playing back and forth, and Malik ran a red light. A truck collided with them, hitting the passenger side of the car. They both had major injuries and were rushed to the hospital. Bria was six months pregnant and lost the baby that night, and ever since then, she's been struggling with this. It happened a little over three years ago, and she still can't come to terms with it.

The entire ordeal was horrific and still put me in my feelings 'til this day. I remember my best friend glowing and looking like a goddess at the most beautiful baby shower, surrounded by so much love. She received so many gifts we had to rent a U-Haul to get them back to their home. When I got the call about the accident, I was a mess. My best friend survived, but their tiny baby didn't make it. We were all so shocked, and I knew no matter what, Bria's life would never be the same.

"Layah, I'm sorry. It's just how I feel. There are so many nights I sit and cry out for my baby girl. The pain is so unbearable, but Malik feels like I should just get over it and just move on." She wiped the tears from her eyes.

"Bri, you know he's not inconsiderate about your feelings. He hurts just like you do over losing her. I overheard him breaking down to his brother many times about her and finding ways to help you. He loves you, sis. You should know that even if you don't know anything else. He's not asking you to forget her; he's just trying to get you to move on and work through the pain. It's almost as if you're still in that moment and time, and you're not. It's been almost four years, which is why he's suggesting counseling for you and him.

He's been so adamant about you two having another baby and finally getting married. I truly believe that this may help you heal. You never have to forget her, but trying to move forward in your life is a must, babe. You can't put a time on your grieving process, but baby, we gotta figure out how to start healing," I expressed to her just as we walked up to our awaiting truck.

"I love Malik, Layah, but I've been battling for years with my thoughts about that night. I have never told anyone this, but I blame him for it all. He's the reason we don't have our daughter. If he wasn't playing with me in the car, he wouldn't have run that light, and we would still have her!" She cried, and all I could do was stand there and watch her. I was in fuckin' shock because all these years, she was sitting there harboring feelings of hate and resentment for a man that loved her effortlessly without limits. I didn't want to see my friend hurt, so I gave her a hug, trying to calm her down and get her into the car. Hearing her say shit like she didn't want to get married was one thing, but to blame him was some shit that could rock him to the core. I knew he blamed himself, but to know that's how she feels about him might be something different.

"Bri, I can't tell you how to feel, but playing with that man's feelings isn't the right thing to do. If you don't plan on forgiving him and marrying him, then I think you need to be honest with him and let him go, babe. You're my best friend, he's my brother-in-law, and I love you both. I don't want to see either of you hurt. Just know that I'm here for you."

Knowing Bria didn't want Malik in the way he wanted her had me stuck. I loved my brother in-law, and I loved my best friend, but being caught in the middle of their relationship was something I didn't want to sign up for. Still, I was here for Bria always, and whatever her decision was going to be regarding Malik, I was rocking with her 'til the wheels fall off.

"I guess I have some things to think about." She gave a half smile, wiping the tears from her eyes as we got into the car to head home. Hearing her confessions got my ass stressed because I knew nothing good was going to come from this shit. Malik is a loose cannon, and even though he loves her, I know this shit is going to drive him overboard. He's done everything to be there for her, and to find out she blames him is going to kill him.

By the time I made it home, it was already a little after four, and I couldn't believe it, but Lynx was still home, and in the family room watching movies with Bray. Being married and moving to Puerto Rico has been a big adjustment for both of us, but we're making it work. I'm always asking him to adjust his schedule to spend more time at home, so him being here today makes me smile. I love my husband, but it's been a strain on our marriage because he's gone all the time. I knew his profession when we got married, but I didn't sign up to be in a marriage and still feel like I'm a single mother. I spend a lot of time at home with our son, and even though we have a nanny for Bray, he's our son to take care of. I have asked him to spend more time at home with us, and that hasn't happened. I would love for him to step down from that life, but I know he wouldn't, so I never asked and probably never will. All I'm asking for is a little time for his wife and child.

"Hey, you two!" I smiled, standing at the doorway. Every time I laid eyes on Lynx, it was as if there was a sharp pain in my windpipe, restricting my breathing. He's the type of fine that has you at a loss for words. Then, our son had his whole face and personality. Everyday our love deepened and intensified. Everything in his manner soothed me. God blessed me when he gave me a tall, sexy, black king that I call my man. I just wanted his fine ass to make more time. Especially with me being all the way in Puerto Rico without the help and support of my family. Hired staff was cool, but still, I needed my husband.

"Hey, pretty lady. How was your day?" Lynx stood up and headed over to me, pulling me into his arms with the biggest smile on his face. That shit melted my heart.

"It was a good day. It's an even better day coming home, and you're still here." Leaning into him, I placed soft kisses on his lips.

"I told you before you left that I wasn't going anywhere. You said let's have a date night, so a date night is what you get. I'm spending time with our son now, and tonight it's me and you, so go relax. We'll leave around eight." He squeezed my ass, and I swear my pussy instantly creamed for this man. He just does it for me. One thing I will say is when he's home, he wears my ass out.

A couple hours later, I was stepping out of the shower, and

Lynx was standing there with a big ass smirk on his face holding his big ass dick in his hand.

"No, babe! I just showered!" The look on his face let me know that he didn't give two shits about what I had to say or that damn shower.

"Then I guess we'll have to shower again because our date starts now. All I want to do is dig in this sweet ass pussy and put a baby in you." He stepped into my personal space, pushing me against the wall. I'd agreed to have another baby, but now that I see he's not a consistent at-home husband and father to the child we have, that shit is on ice. I'm not having another baby with him until he's home more to help with raising of our children. The damn nannies didn't have them, we did, and it's our job to nurture, raise, and protect them. So, I'm going to continue to pop these birth control pills, and his ass can continue to work at putting a baby in me.

He jolted me from my thoughts as soon as he placed one hand around my neck while easing the other one over my clit. His fingers slid over my soaking wet pussy.

"Just let it happen, lil mama!" His voice tickled my ear, which had my ass dripping something crazy. Even though I feel the way I do about him not being home, when it comes to pleasing me, he had my ass screaming for the dick one minute and crying for him to remove it the next. And tonight, wouldn't be any different. I love having sex with my husband, so I'm never turning down the chance to get bent over. He just could've did this shit before I took my damn shower. Lynx and I didn't care where we were. If we wanted to fuck, that's what we were going to do.

"Ahhh fuck!" I cried out from the sensation I was feeling. Lynx could blow in my direction, and my pussy would answer him before I did. Sliding my hands down to his dick, I gripped it in my hand, causing him to graze his teeth across my neck. He was nibbling and sucking on it as if tonight was our last time together.

"Fuck!" He gritted as his fingers slid in and out of me, and that shit had a bitch shedding tears and trembling so badly.

"Babe! Pleaassseee!" I begged, grinding my pussy hard as shit on his fingers because my ass was on the verge of exploding. And he knew that shit. It never failed with me. The moment this man touched me, it was always tears and shaking like a crackhead needing a fix.

"Get that nut, lil mama," he gritted, and just as I started cumming, he slid the head of his dick across my wet pussy. That shit sent me over the top as I cried out, but my cries got caught in my throat the moment he pushed inside of me. I was full of tears, and I felt as if I was stuck in place.

"Let that shit go, baby girl!" He moved in and out of me so hard that all I could do was hold on for the ride. You would've thought this man was hurting me the way I was crying and moaning right now.

"Oh shit, Lynx!" I moaned.

"I can't get enough of this pussy!" he growled as he fucked and carried me to the bed all at the same damn time. When it came to his fuck game, my husband was a problem. A problem

I don't think I ever wanted to fix. I got an instant attitude when he pulled out of me to lay me on the bed and was happy as fuck the moment he slid back inside me. It's toxic sexual behavior for me, and I love that shit. Call me a professional in the day and a pussy popper for this nigga at night. As much as I love fucking my husband, I could never handle this dick. My ass was always running, and he was always tearing my ass in two because he knew I couldn't take the way he gave it up.

"Stop trying to run and take this dick!" He slapped me on the ass as he pounded the fuck out of me. That one move had my ass putting the dick in a chokehold and squirting so bad I felt like I was going to pass out.

"Got damn, this pussy good as fuck!" He gripped my ass, spread my cheeks apart, and tore my life the fuck up.

"Fuckkkk!" He growled as he filled me up with his cum. It took a minute to catch our breath, and a few minutes later, he pulled me out of bed to go shower. A couple of hours later, we were dressed and on our way to my favorite restaurant Zanzzy's. It was an upscale seafood restaurant, and the food was amazing. Lynx placed a call to the restaurant to let them know we were coming, and they said they would have a table ready for us. A few minutes later, we were walking into the restaurant with our security detail behind us. Because of who he was, we had to have security with us at all times, which took a minute for me to get used to. I've always been around a lot of security when it came to Uncle Juelz and my Kassom family, but we've never personally had it. As goofy as my dad is, he's never played about his family being protected.

When he said he had us, that's what he meant, and we believed him.

"Welcome back, Mr. and Mrs. Carter. We have your table ready. Right this way." She smiled as one of our guards stepped ahead of Lynx, and the other one walked behind me. The waitress seated us and then seated the guards at the table next to us.

After taking our drink orders, she said our waiter would be out to take our food orders shortly. Ten minutes later, the waiter was back to take our order.

"We have a blackened sea bass and garlic and herb trout sautéed in a white wine sauce. What can I get started for you both tonight?" He turned in the direction of Lynx, who wasted no time placing our orders.

"I'll have the surf & turf, and the beautiful lady will have the seafood dinner." Lynx closed his menu, reaching across to grab mine, and handed it to the waiter.

"Yes sir, I'll get this started for you right away." He smiled and walked off to put our orders in. This time out was much needed. I'm hoping he makes this a habit because I'm not sure how much more I could really take. In my profession, time isn't always on my side, but I make that shit happen because I love my husband and son. Just as the waiter came back with our drinks and placed them down, a beautiful woman tried to approach the table, but our guards stopped her. It looked as if she had guards of her own.

"Lynx Carter! What a surprise seeing you here. It's been a while. It's really not a surprise; I knew you would be here. The shit just sounded good saying it. I've tried reaching out to you, yet my attempts have gone unanswered. You always change up when you have something new to play with. I see you've decided to playhouse and marry this one. I was alright with you just sliding your dick in them and leaving these bitches, but to marry one... that's cute. Is she the reason you haven't returned any of my calls or accepted any of my father's invitations for dinner!" The way this bitch approached us had me ready to fuck her ass up.

"Lynx, who the fuck is this bitch?! And why is she standing here like she's some damn Queen of Sheba, thinking she can disrespect me! You better deal with this hoe and get her out of my space!" I spat. I was pissed the hell off.

Seeing a gorgeous girl have my husband tensing had my nostrils flaring as anger filled my damn body. I didn't know who this bitch was, but I was ten-second away from mopping the floor of this nice ass restaurant with her long black hair. Bitch!

He pulled me into his arms and whispered in my ear. "Bring that shit down when talking to me and straighten your crown, Queen. Never let a nothing ass bitch that wishes she was you come to us and shake shit up. She's nobody to me. Just a chick I fucked a few times before I reconnected with you. In public, we're a unit, and as a unit, we stand ten fuckin' toes down for one another.

In private, you can get your shit off all you want! There isn't shit going on with her, and my word to you should be all that matters!" Lynx's tone was calm in spite of his anger. I bit down on my bottom lip to calm my anger as he pinched the bridge of his nose and turned back in her direction.

"Natalie, I don't know what the fuck you have up your sleeve, but know I'm not here to play with you. My wife is off limits, and that shit isn't up for discussion. If you call her anything other than her name, I'ma make you eat them mutha-fuckin' words. Just know I don't play about her, so tread the fuck lightly. Why are you here, and what the fuck do you want with me? I thought telling you we were done and me cutting all ties with your organization was enough."

"I-" she started, but my husband lifted his hand to silence her.

"We were not a couple! I didn't make you any promises, so I don't owe you shit! I didn't feel the need to answer your calls or accept invitations to your dinner events. It's never been like that with us, and you know that shit!" He spat in her direction.

You could tell his words hurt her, but she quickly shook it off, clearing her throat and lifting her head high. Whoever this bitch was, she exuded money. I'd been around enough of the wealthy with my own family to know when a person had it like that. And from the way her designer clothes fit her perfect body as if it was painted on, I knew this bitch was somebody. I couldn't even pinpoint her perfume, so it had to be custom.

"I won't hold you up for too long. I just figured since you're out here parading around with your new family and shit that, I would make a few little adjustments. I've decided to add to that budding household of yours." She raised her hand as if she was waving someone over. A few minutes later, a woman appeared with a beautiful little girl who resembled my husband and son a lot. Seeing her damn near knocked the air out of my body because what is this bitch trying to say? 'Cause I know she's not saying this little girl is Lynx's child.

I blinked a few times and even pinched my skin to make sure I wasn't dreaming, and sure as shit stank, I was wide the fuck awake. Not only was the little girl beautiful and clad in her little Chanel dress and matching Mary Jane shoes, her ass had my baby boy's ENTIRE face. Sweat beads formed on my hairline as my heartbeat sped up hard as fuck, and my breathing became ragged. The silence between all of us, including the guards became unbearable. In that moment, I wanted to be everywhere but in this muthafucka.

"What the fuck! Nat, please don't tell me you did some fuck shit like this!" Lynx blurted with a mug on his face, and I knew then he was about to turn this place out.

"What the hell is going on?" I questioned because my husband seemed to be stuck.

"Since we all can't put this shit together, I'll do it for you. Lynx, this is our daughter Siani. I was fine keeping her a secret and letting you live your life, but I be damned, if I'm going to let you live your happily ever after, with your wife and son and think you're going to leave my daughter out. Nah, baby boy, we're not doing that." She chuckled.

"So, you're pinning a kid on my husband because he's moved on? I know your type; you're out here sleeping with any baller you can get your hooks into just so that you can get a payday. My husband ain't claiming no damn body or paying shit without a DNA test!" I stepped in her personal space, ready to beat her ass.

31

"Baller? Payday? Is this chick serious right now?! Baby girl, let me bring you up to speed, so that we're all on the same page. I probably have more money than yo' nigga, and let's just say the power we both hold, can go pound for pound. I think it's best you sit this one out, wifey, while I address our man!" She smiled over at me, and before I knew it, my fist connected with that hoe's mouth.

"I don't give a fuck who you are, nor do I give a fuck about your power! Bitch, I will beat your ass in this damn restaurant." Lynx pulled me back, trying to calm me down. He nodded for the guards to come closer to me, and when they did, he turned to face this bitch, Natalie.

"Nat, you know who I am and everything I'm capable of. Yeah, you know! You and your pop have always needed my organization to handle all the shit that y'all couldn't. So, you know it's up when I turn the heat up. Don't fuck with me and get yo' ass touched. How the fuck you think you're just gonna pop up and say this little girl is mine?

I haven't been with your ass in five years or more. And you wait until now to approach me, all over some jealousy shit?! I could kill yo' ass right now for playing in my damn face. I take care of what's mine, and what's mine is the kid I have with my fuckin' wife. Like she said, ain't shit moving without a DNA test. All I know is, you better pray this kid doesn't come back to be mine. I'ma kill you, and that's a promise, 'cause don't fuck with me like that.

I'll never deny a child that belongs to me, but you deserve a bullet for this shit! We'll set that shit up, and I'll be in touch with a place and time. Now, get the fuck outta my face!" The veins were protruding from my husband's neck, and I knew he was ready to explode.

"DNA! You can look at her and tell that she's your daughter. My daughter is five years old, nigga. She belongs to you, and that's all I'm going to say about that. I think it's best that we finish this conversation at my hotel. Say goodbye to your wife, and I'll see you soon, daddy." This bitch done lost her fucking mind, thinking she gon' keep talking crazy, and I let that shit slide. My mama's name is Gia, and my dad is Gabe; I'm about to rock this bitch! The minute I made a move, her security stepped in front of her, and mine was pulling me back.

"Lynx, is she serious right now? Could this be possible?" I asked him because the little girl just stood there watching it all go down with tears in her eyes. I'm a mother first, and I would hate it if my son witnessed some shit like this. I was pissed the fuck off and ready to fuck her ass up, but they wouldn't let me get at her ass.

When shit is peaceful, it's always that one muthafucka that will come and try to knock you off your shit. I couldn't believe that this shit was even happening right now. I was the fuck pissed, and I was ready to go in on his ass too. Like, what the fuck is really going on here? She stepped closer to him and whispered something in his ear. It was as if the blood drained from his body, and he was standing there as if he was paralyzed.

"Lynx, what's wrong? What did she say?" I touched his arms to gain his attention, hoping he would snap out of it.

"Layah, I gotta handle this shit. Go home, and I'll explain

everything when I get there." And then he walked out behind her. I could feel the tears burning my eyes, but I refused to let them fall. With renewed humiliation, I tore my eyes away from my man walking out of the restaurant with a bitch and child like they were one big happy ass family. I was embarrassed as fuck, so I paid the bill and left the restaurant.

CHAPTER 4

Lynx

I'm still trying to process what this bitch said to me, and I couldn't even deal with the hurt that was written all over my wife's face. I had to handle this shit. There was no waiting to figure things out, I had to be on top of it now. Good thing my security detail has more than one vehicle. By the time I made it outside, her detail had already pulled off. I hopped in my awaiting truck and my driver sped off. I sent my wife a text because she needed to know that I truly had to take care of this shit now.

> Malayah: You know I would never disrespect you like that, but I had to leave and talk to her. I will explain it as soon as I get home, babe. I love you.

I was hoping she responded, but she never did, and I pray she understood. I shot Malik and Nori a text as well.

> Malik, Nori: We have a big problem; I'll hit your line asap. Just know Nat is in town, and she's on some major bullshit. I'm at her hotel now.

> Malik: Send me your location, and if I don't hear from you in thirty, I'm coming. Bro, I'm serious check in in thirty.

When I say this bitch is on some bullshit, that's exactly what the fuck I mean. The shit she just told me was my one-way ticket to the fuckin' chair, and unfortunately, I'm not the only one. I had an idea of where she could be staying. When Natalie and her father are in town, it's only one hotel they stay in and that's the Hotel Camina. As soon as we pulled into the parking lot, I jumped out and headed inside with a couple of my men behind me. Just like I figured, her guards were in the lobby. A few of her men led me to her floor, tapped on the door, and they opened it to let only me inside. I assured Tony that I would be fine, and they waited outside the door.

"I'm glad you saw things my way." She walked over to the bar to fix a drink. She tried to pass one to me, and I didn't want shit this bitch was serving.

"This shit isn't a game! You know I'm going to kill you, right? It may not be today or tomorrow, but I'm going to make you suffer, bitch. I'm not going to even talk to you about this kid situation right now." I was ready to snap this bitch's neck.

Nat and her pop were some dirty muthafuckas, and I'm still trying to figure out why I started fuckin' with her ass in the first place. I let a fat ass and good pussy cloud my judgement. Now that shit gon' cost me in a major way.

"Shit, you should've learned being in this game. First rule is never let your opponent catch yo' bitch ass slipping. Like I told you earlier, I have proof that you ordered the hit on the judge, the prosecutor, and that federal agent nigga that you were tussling with over your needy-looking ass wife. I thought you were going to come stronger than that. I'll give it to you, though. She's definitely a beautiful woman, but she's not me. She doesn't fit you. You need someone on your arm that exudes not only beauty but power, and wealth, and we both know that's me. I'm from the streets; my father built our organization with his blood, sweat, and tears.

He has groomed me to run the Alvarez Cartel when he decides to step down. I'll be the sole heir, and you and I together could be unstoppable. I'm sorry I didn't tell you about her, but I did attempt to get in touch with you. When I found out that you had gotten married and had a son, I was pissed. Let's be real, Lynx. Your ass ghosted me and cut all dealings with my dad. He even called you a few months ago asking for your help and you refused to help him. Now we on some get back. Now you gotta play by my fuckin' rules. If not, you and your lil' lawyer wife gon' do that bid together, 'cause the shit I got on y'all, it's the chair for sure.

Oh yeah, you didn't think I would leave her out, now did you? It can be me and you against the world. Nah, it's going to be me and you against the world because I know you're not gonna let her lil' pretty ass sit. And I don't like her attitude, so I want you with me. That's the rules to this shit or the Feds gon' get everything I got!" She sipped her drink, looking over at me with this fucked up ass smirk on her face.

"What the fuck!" I yelled. Somebody in my camp had to be helping her ass 'cause she has too much information on me. I'm careful with everything I do, but this bitch definitely got to somebody. I can promise you this, I won't rest until I find out who the disloyal muthafucka is.

"I knew this wouldn't be the last time I seen or heard from you. Never would I have imagined you would come to me on some blackmail shit. I didn't leave on bad terms with you; our business relationship with you and your pop wasn't on bad terms. It just ran its course and ended, but now you're so-called hiding a kid that you say belongs to me. That shit doesn't make sense, and it damn sure doesn't add up.

Now you're so-called mad because I got married and have a child? Bitch, I was blowing your fuckin' back out and that's as far as that shit goes. You know this some bullshit, right? And you know damn well you're not fucking with some nigga off the streets, right? I'm not leaving my muthafuckin' wife for you and no other bitch!" This bitch was crazy as hell if she thought I was going to just give in to her ass.

She lifted a remote from the bar and turned on the television.

"Oh, you're going to leave her. Trust me, baby boy. You don't want to make that little boy of yours an orphan, now do you?" I ignored her and kept my eyes on the screen. Seconds later, different scenes started playing. One of those was of me and the Kassom crew inside that nigga Naiem's crib when we took him and his wife out. Everyone was in the video at some point. Juelz, Gabe, Truth, Jah, Ju Ju, Me, Malik, Nori, Mel, a few of my guards, and Kari and her crew. This shit was all bad!

"Slice that nigga's head and send it to his bitch ass son!" It was a video of me giving the order. She even had Nori when he took out the judge and prosecutor. My knees buckled, 'cause this bitch could bring us all down with the click of a button.

This bitch could not only take me down, my wife, and my operation, but she could take down the Kassom family and their organization. I could feel the rage inside of me, and there was nothing I could do to stop it. I wanted this bitch's head; all I could see was murder, and before I knew it, I was on her ass. Wrapping my hands around her throat, I tried to choke the life outta her ass. Her guards tried to pull me off her, and that shit wasn't happening. The only way they were going to get me off of her was to kill my ass. I felt a sharp pain to my side and realized they were tasing my ass. Only that caused me to let go. She fell to the floor gasping for air, and I was still trying to get out of their hold and get to her ass.

"You fuckin' dirty bitch! You better pray that I don't find a way out of this shit because your death is going to be one that they talk about for years to come. Fucking with me is already a fucked-up move, but coming for the Kassom's only adds to the bomb that's about to come down on you. You don't know this family the way you think you do.

39

Their reach is just as wide as mine, and the connections they have could bury you and your pop! Hell, my organization alone could do that to you, so it has to be something bigger than you wanting to be with me. What else is it?!" I roared. I just couldn't believe this bitch would stoop to this level just to get me in her bed.

I know she couldn't have come up with this shit alone. She had to have had some kind of help. I'm not sure if her Pop would even come up with something like this. I'm not sure who all is behind this, but you better know I'm going to find out and put all them bitches in the ground! The Alvarez Cartel is one of the largest Cartels in Mexico, but they had nothing on the Carter Cartel or the Vega Cartel, which is now owned by the Kassom family. Santiago Vega handed his organization over to his grandsons years ago. She doesn't know this, but the Carter Cartel is now connected and running the Vega Cartel as well.

The only reason this bitch has me by the balls is because she has my wife, my brother, cousins, and my wife's family tied up in this shit. If it was just me, we could go to war, and may the best muthafucka win, but this bitch is unstable, so I have to play her game. You better know everything I do comes with a plan. Nat has a black mom and a Mexican pop, so she thinks that she's this connected down ass chick, but don't know shit about the hood.

Her mom is from the streets of New York, and was a money hungry bitch that got hooked up with Alonzo Alvarez. Supposedly when she got pregnant with Nat, he wifed her ass up. Fuckkkkkk!

"I'm going to let you have that one. I know all this shit I'm telling you is a hard pill to digest. Lynx, I know you're pissed 'cause after tonight, your life will change forever. We're bringing all of our allies together to form the strongest and deadliest Cartel to ever exist. Oh yeah, don't think I don't know why you've been hanging with Santiago Vega's people. Imagine my excitement when I found out that I got those niggas by their dicks. Juelz Kassom has been walking around for years like his ass couldn't be touched!

Trust me when I say my pussy creams knowing I'm about to touch the hem of that nigga's tailored suit. Yeah, I know the Kassom family all too well, and I hate everything they bitch asses stand for! Years ago, my dad went to Santiago and tried to join forces with him, and he basically laughed in his face! And now it's checkmate, bitch!" I couldn't believe this shit was happening right now!

"I'ma take great pleasure in killing you, bitch," I whispered and sealed that shit with a forehead kiss. I have no choice but to agree to the shit she wants until I get my hands on the videos. I'ma do what she wants; I don't have a choice. One thing I'ma always do is carry this shit on my back and come out on top. This predicament we're in is no fuckin' different.

"I'll do you a favor, babe. You can take a few days to get your personal shit in order. A copy of that video has been sent to your phone for your personal use. Get it out of your head; killing me is out of the question. There are several copies of this video, and they're in the hands of some of my most trusted people. Do what I've asked of you, and the day you marry me and sign your organizations over to me is the day you get every-thing I have on all of you. I'll be here waiting for you to return, but don't get cute and try to be a hero because you won't win." She turned and walked out of the room, and I just stood in place as her guards awaited my next move.

My phone kept going off, and I knew it was my brother. I forgot to call him back, so I headed for the door to leave. By the time I made it down to the lobby, Malik and our security was coming through the doors. He wasn't playing about me calling in thirty, I loved the fuck outta my brother.

"What the fuck is going on? You good?" He asked, walking up to me.

"Bro, it's all bad. We gotta get the fuck outta here." I moved to the door, and we headed out to the parking lot. When Malik and I got into my truck, I pulled the video up and passed it to him.

"Yo, what the fuck! The fuck did she get this shit from? Nigga, this could get us the fuckin' chair! What does she want?" He looked at me, and anger was the only thing evident in his eyes right now.

"She wants me. She wants me to marry her and sign over the organization. She said her daughter is mine. I'm not sure if that's the case, but the little girl does look like me and Bray." I shrugged.

"What! Nah, bro, we not going out like that. This bitch gotta go, and whatever she got on us, we can get that shit back. You're fuckin' married already, so what the fuck she wants you to leave sis to be with her?" He asked, but he already knew the answer to that.

"Yeah, and that's exactly what I have to do. At least what I have to make it seem like. I'm going to do what I have to do to save my wife and the rest of y'all. I'm not going to lie down and take the shit. You know me, and you know how we roll. I just can't take any chances; she has too much on all of us.

I know you ready to go to war for this, and so am I, but until we know how to get out of this and be sure of it. We gotta move in silence. Trust me, I'm strapping my boots up and carrying this load on my back. She gave me three days, so I'm heading home to talk to Malayah and then off to New York. They all deserve to know what we're up against." I sighed, and the more I thought about it, the more fucked up this shit is. Breaking my wife's heart was the last thing I ever wanted to do because I knew she wouldn't understand it. But I'll always do what I have to do to protect her and my son. She better know that I'm going to do everything to fight my way out of this shit and back to her. Right now, I need them safe, and the safest thing for her is to be in New York with her family.

"Bro, what the fuck are you saying! Do you know what the fuck this will do to your wife? What will this do to your mental? What the fuck about you? I'm not about to let you go with this bitch like it's all good. Fuck that! If she wants it with us, we gon' give that hairy, big back bitch what the fuck she looking for! She gave you three days, and we gon' take all of them muthafuckas. I'm with whatever you got to do for now, but if you explain this shit to Malayah, I'm sure she would understand.

This shit is fucked up, and I truly wanna take my guards in that muthafucka guns blazing and paint that bitch brains on the wall like a Picasso painting. Fuckkk! This bitch got me fucked up! Man, hit me with a wheel's up time." He dapped me up and got out of the car. My driver pulled off, and we headed back to my house. We were pulling into the driveway thirty minutes later, but I had to sit here for a few minutes and collect my thoughts. Because I knew it was about to be an emotional ass rollercoaster with my wife. Never in a million years would I think that I could ever hurt her the way shit was about to go down. Getting out of the car and walking inside, I knew she was in our bedroom because the downstairs lights were off.

"Dad, call me back." I heard her say, and I assumed that she was leaving her dad a message. She stopped in her tracks when she saw me standing in the doorway.

"Oh, so you decided to come home to the fuckin' wife you left in the middle of the got damn restaurant! You embarrassed the hell out of me, and yet you go run behind another bitch! I don't give a fuck what she's claiming you have with her; you take care of home first!" I can understand her anger.

"Layah, calm down and let me talk to you. The shit she whispered to me is why I walked out to meet with her. She has so much shit on us that shit could put us under the jail or in the chair. You gotta know that I would never do anything to hurt you intentionally, babe. But uhhh... ummm... I have to handle this with her, and in order to do that, I have to move in with her. She wants me to marry her and sign over my organization. I'm going to do everything I can to get out of this, but for now, this is the move. This is what I have to do. Just know I love the fuck outta you, Layah! I love my son, but I gotta tame this bitch because it's so many lives that are hanging on the edge because of her, and I'm the only one that can fix this shit." I walked over to her, trying to grab her hand, but she snatched away from me.

"What! Are you leaving me for her? You're Lynx Fuckin' Carter! fix this shit! We have a fucking son, Lynx!" She screamed, running up on me and hitting me in the chest as she broke down in my arms. Seeing her like this crushed me. I love this woman with everything in me. She's my fuckin' reason!

"I'm sorry, baby. I gotta do this shit for the family until I can figure this thing out and get everyone cleared from this. I gotta do it. Protecting you and my son will always be my first priority. I don't know if her daughter is my child, but I'm going to find out. Shit with me Natalie was never serious; she was something to do. I helped her pop's organization out, and shit popped off with me and her from there. I've always been a man about my shit. I would never lie to you about anything or give you a reason to question my shit. She has all of our lives in the palm of her hands, and that includes you, babe." I sighed, and I could see her fighting with her thoughts internally.

"Layah, she has me on video ordering the hit on the judge, that nigga's mom, and footage of us killing them inside the house when we rescued you. You're connected to Naeim, and you were in the house when we took him out," I revealed. She stood there as her body shook from the thunderous cry she let

45

out, and I just couldn't get over the fact that we were going through this shit right now.

"So, are we really doing this, Lynx?" She looked at me. I could see the pain in her face, but there wasn't anything I could do to soothe her.

"That's how it has to be for now. I'd rather see you and my son safe, happy, and living a carefree life. I promise when I fix this shit, I'm coming back to get my wife and child." When I attempted to pull her into my arms, she started becoming erratic, swinging on me, and I knew this was out of hurt.

"Nah, nigga! Don't bother coming for me, 'cause if you can't fight for me and protect us here with you now, stay the fuck away from me! You're supposed to be that nigga, yet you're letting this bitch call the muthafuckin' shots and threaten our livelihood!" She screamed as she rushed into her closet and started throwing her clothes inside. I let out a deep sigh, trying to calm myself.

I knew if I didn't, things would get crazy. I didn't want to take anything out on her because this wasn't on her. It was on me. As I walked into my closet to pack a bag, I wasn't sure when I would come back here. I know she's hurt, but I be damned if I'm going to let Nat hurt my family because of some shit that was all on me. They're in this situation because this bitch is fuckin' delusional.

I'ma always go to war for mine, so shit gotta be this way for now. Natalie can cause a lot of damage. Right now, Malayah isn't looking at the bigger picture because her feelings are hurt, and that's all she cares about. I had to get my mental together so that I could come up with a plan. I think it's best if we headed to New York tonight, so I finished packing my bags. Then I texted Nori to set up a meeting with Juelz and his crew tomorrow and let them know it's an urgent matter. After I sent him the text, I walked out of my closet, and she was standing there with a face full of tears.

"Why the fuck is she doing this? What does she want from us to keep what she has to herself? If it's money, give it to her. How could you think this shit is ok to just end your marriage and leave your wife and child!"

"Me! She wants me, Malayah! Natalie is wealthy; she's the next in line for her father's organization, the Alvarez Cartel. Baby, I have the power to do a lot of things, and who I am can move some shit, but this bitch has us all hanging off the ledge. One wrong move, and that's it! She wants me to marry her and sign over my operation. You're a defense attorney; you know how this shit goes." I made a promise to myself that I would give her the facts straight and not beat around the bush with her.

She didn't even respond. She wiped the tears from her eyes, grabbed her bags, and walked out of our bedroom. I swear seeing her walk away seemed as if someone slowly eased a knife in my fuckin' heart. I have never in my life felt that type of pain. I took a few minutes to get myself together and then sent Malik a text to meet me at the jet hangar.

CHAPTER 5
Malayah

The pain that was ripping through me damn near suffocated me. It was as if I was living in a damn twilight zone. My husband of almost four years was telling me that he was leaving me. That was hard as fuck to hear, especially from Lynx. I loved my husband, and I thought he loved me the same way. There is nothing or no one that could come in and make me leave my family. My phone started ringing, and I really didn't feel like talking to anyone, but it was Bria calling.

"Hello." I answered the call because I didn't want her worrying about me and Bray.

"Layah, are you alright? Malik told me what was going on; he just left to head to New York. Security has been beefed up and my damn house looks like the president is here visiting."

"Things are really bad! He told me has to move in with her!

She wants him to marry her, and if he has to, that's what he's going to do!" I cried.

"Layah, let's give them a chance to figure things out. Malik told me everything and said he saw the video. That bitch has a lot on all of them, and I think maybe Lynx is just moving off of emotions right now. Just know that he's not with her; they're on their way to New York. Do you need me to come over there with you?"

"No, I'm headed to the J.W Marriott near the airport. Me and Bray are catching a flight home to my parents in the morning. I'm moving out of the house. If he wants this marriage over, I'm going to give him what he wants. I guess it's a good thing when you're married to an attorney that doesn't need shit from you. This divorce should be quick and easy. Zayah is the best at it, and I know she will process this quickly," I told her.

"Do what you need to do for you, sis. I just think you need to wait and see what happens. I wish I could leave with y'all, but I have a client in the morning. Damn, this is all so fucked up. I wish it was something I could do for you, friend. When I'm finished here, I'll be heading to New York. I'll be staying with Aunt Nae."

"Call me when you get in town. I'll be at my parents' house until I figure things out." We said our goodbyes and ended the call.

My flight landed in New York at JFK an hour ago, and Bray and I were now on our way to my parents' house. I decided to just talk to them once I got home. I have been up crying all damn morning, not believing all of the shit that happened yesterday. I mean, our day started off so damn positive and beautiful and ended in some bullshit.

"Yayyyy, it's Pop-Pop's house!" Bray started clapping as we pulled up to the gates. He loves my dad! He loves his mom-mom, but my dad was his best friend, and all my dad did was talk shit to my baby. Bray didn't even care. Anything his pop-pop said he thought was funny, and he would just fall out laughing. I love this little boy's entire life, and he has no clue that our lives are going to be different without his dad.

Once we got through the security process, the gates opened, and a few minutes later, we were pulling up to the house. The driver helped me get the bags out of the car; I just had the driver sit everything at the door. I could get my dad to get them once he calmed down from the fact that we were moving back in. The door clicked after I entered my code. I was happy as hell the pin was still the same because my dad was an advocate of changing shit around to keep us out of the house. True story, I think his ass really don't want us to come visit.

Music was playing when I opened the door, and it was the damn song, *Woman to Woman* by Shirley Brown playing. I haven't seen his ass yet, and I was ready to punch him in his damn throat with his old ass.

"Gia, you heard what Shirley told Barbara! I know that's right, Shirley! You better let her ass know!" My dad sang out loud, gyrating his body to the song while cooking.

"Oh, my goodness, what are y'all doing home!" My mom jumped up in excitement, and my dad turned in our direction.

"Pop-Pop!" Brayden yelled out and took off running towards my dad.

"Ahhhh hell nawl! What the hell is going on? Didn't I tell you to let me know when you and this demon seed decide to come visit? I really do think it's best that y'all get a hotel and let me and your mama come visit y'all over there. It works best for me 'cause I just don't have time to be going back and forth with this lil' nigga and his spirits. I think y'all should only visit, but maybe twice a year, and I prefer it to be in the winter 'cause hell is hottt! Them niggas like to play on hell temperatures; they don't like that cold shit.

I'm glad Ma gave me some jugs of that holy oil to splash on his ass when he comes to visit. I think his lil' ass left some spirits in that damn room of his the last time he was here. I went in there to put some clothes in the drawers, and I swear a lil' nigga walked out of the closet throwing up gang signs. I left the fuckin' room and them damn clothes, right the fuck there. Gia can go in there and play with them niggas, but you won't catch Gabe in there. Then this lil' nigga be walking around the house at night like his ass is possessed when he's here. Don't nobody got time for that shit.

I can't be looking out for them damn UFO's they say been flying around and keeping my damn eyes on his ass. He like that lil' girl from that old ass movie... Gia, what's that lil' crazy heifer name that's constantly staring at the fuckin' TV?...Caroline! That's her damn name! *'Get out the light, Carolineeee!'* Hell nawl! If I tell this lil' nigga to get out the light and this lil' cock-eyed ass nigga start twirling his lil' muthafuckin' neck and head in a circle, he gotta go!

That lil' nigga got one time, and I'ma sit his ass out the door and call his cartel-ish ass daddy to come get him! Better yet, why don't y'all sleep in the pool house? Your mama went to Macy's and got some stuff to fix it up the other day." It was hard to be damn sad around my dad. I couldn't help but to laugh at his ass. But he gon' leave my damn son alone.

"Dad, you know he sleepwalks! Leave my son alone!"

"Pop-Pop, I luh you!" Bray giggled, wrapping his little frail arms around my dad's leg.

"Hell nawl! Get off me, Satan!" My dad lifted his leg and started shaking it to get Bray off, and I had to laugh because Brayden thought it was so funny.

"Where is Lynx? Is he traveling?" My mom looked over at me, and that's when she noticed my appearance and my swollen eyes from all the crying I had done.

"I'm not sure where he's at, being as though we're no longer together and getting a divorce," I said to her, and my dad's neck snapped back so fast I thought he broke that shit.

"Divorced! Mmmm Mmmm! Hell nawl, this ain't that. I done told y'all when you feel the need to come home, DON'T! Even if you and your sister leave these niggas, y'all still rich. Gon' on over to your sister house and take the seed of Chucky

THE CARTER CARTEL: LYNX CARTER

mixed with the Spawn with yo' ass. Mano done bought that big ass house, and y'all got plenty of room to live happily ever the fuck after over there. Me and yo' mama done did our job! That's raise y'all asses to get gangstas and Cartel-ish niggas that got the Federales watching his ass.

Mano loves his brother-in-law, always talking about Lynx's black ass. I told the nigga to keep on hanging with his bro-bro, he gon' be doing 90 to life, and his new girl gone be Dorianisha. While my baby out here in the real world crying free my baby 'til it's backwards! I tried to teach y'all, but you were definitely listening to your mama. You should've been trying CiCi lil' prayer she was doing. 'Cause that Gi Gi prayer your mama taught you didn't do you so good. Your mama got lucky 'cause true enough, she was out here trying to catch her a thug a two, and God blessed her real good with my ass. That's my dude. You know God is good, and he's always on time.

See, I'ma different type of thug. I take pride in my street dealings, and I'm careful. God took his time with me, baby. God said I'ma make you a drug dealer and rich, but you gon' be one of those ones, and I said, yesssuhhh, I trust you, Lord! And look at me now! Y'all should've come to me instead of your mama! Did you at least hit up that nigga I sent you from the Escobar Cartel? He on the lighter side, and I know how you love them lil' chocolate niggas, but his money green. I think he might have more than Lynx's ass." This man was indeed crazy. Ma really should get him checked out.

"Pop-popppp!" Bray wanted my dad to pick him up, but this dude just stared at him like his lil' ass was stink.

"Nahhh, this not gon' work for me! The hell you mean, y'all getting a damn divorce? I told you them Cartel niggas switch up just like these IG influencers switch niggas." He shook his head as he plated the food he was cooking.

"What happened, baby?" My mom looked at me, waiting for me to explain.

"Gia, if the nigga-"

"There is another woman! She has a little girl, and she said it's Lynx's daughter. She's threatening him with some heavy stuff. She said she has him ordering the hit on the judge, and she has information on Dad, Uncle Juelz, Zelan, and Uncle Truth! Information that could send everyone to jail for a very long time. He said he has to give her what she wants in order to protect me and everyone else." We heard a loud noise crashing to the floor, and my dad had dropped the plate he was holding.

"She got what on who?!" My dad yelled, pulling his phone out of his pocket and dialing a number.

"I'm in the city. I was just about to call you, but I guess Malayah is there and explained it to you. I set up a meeting with Juelz, so I'm sure he's going to call you as well. I'll be over to his crib in an hour," Lynx got out before Dad could even get anything out.

"Bruh, she said this chick got some shit on us. How bad is it?" Dad asked him.

"The death penalty bad. See you in an hour." The call dropped, and my dad's knees damn near buckled.

"Ohhh My Fucking God!" My mom cried out, and that caused me to shed more tears.

"Fuckkkkkkkk!" My dad screamed out, and that shit broke me. Never would I think me dealing with a man would bring this kind of trouble to my family. I loved my parents, and to see them broken and scared is something I never wanted to witness. I'm hurt about losing my husband and wish that he chose me over that bitch, but I guess it is what it is.

"Dad, I got you. Just as long as I have air in my body, I'll defend you until I don't have air to breathe. You don't have the best defense attorney in the US as a daughter for nothing." I walked over to hug him and my mom. Then I pulled my phone out and sent Lynx a text.

> Me: I need all the information you have on that bitch!

Husbae: Done. I love you.

I didn't even bother responding to his ass because I had nothing to say. I grabbed my crying son and headed upstairs to put him in his bedroom. He was upset because my mom and dad were upset. I had to find a way to fix this shit because my family doesn't deserve this shit.

CHAPTER 6
Gabe

All that joking shit went out the window 'cause I need to know what the fuck this so-called bitch had on me and my fuckin' family! Playing with us has never been a safe thing to do. Just because we're older ain't shit changed but the muthafuckin time and year. Them guns still bust the same way! I was on my way to pick up Truth so that we could meet up with the family. This shit was insane! Out of all the shit we've done and even the shit that went down with Juelz a few years ago, we've never been caught up in no shit! The family, down to the kids, have always been careful when it came to the family business. So, to hear that some bitch got information on us, is mind-boggling as fuck. Like, a whole bitch was threatening to infiltrate us. A bitch that I have never even seen before. My mind was running a marathon during my drive, trying to figure out how the hell we didn't know we were being recorded.

My phone lit up, and it was Ju sending out a text letting us know that we needed to meet at his house asap. I responded, letting him know that I was already getting Truth and we would be there soon. My fuckin' head was pounding with the way my thoughts were playing hopscotch. How did Lynx even let this bitch get so close to his organization that she was able to corner us like this? I needed the back story on this chick, and I needed that shit asap. Snapping from my thoughts, I pulled up to Truth's security gate. And to my surprise, this nigga was outside of the gate waiting on me.

"Nigga, I said we might go to the penitentiary for the rest of our life. That didn't mean you start practicing on how to walk the yard yet. The fuck wrong with you? It's hot as hell out here, and that walk from your house to this gate, gotta be a good five miles." I was looking at this nigga like he was crazy. The way sweat littered his forehead and the neck of his t-shirt, I knew he was burning the fuck up.

"Shut your ass up and drive." Truth dapped me up when he got inside, and I made a U-turn to head to Juelz's crib. Thirty minutes later, we were walking inside Juelz's home, and everyone was already there, including Ma Lai, Pop Santiago, JuJu, Kari, and Jah.

There weren't any jokes, no laughing and no monkey business like it normally was. That shit let me know that everyone was concerned. Hell, I wanted to comment on Ma wearing that hot ass black hoodie, fuckin' polka dot shorts, and rain boots without a lick of clouds or rain in the sky, but I wasn't even in a damn joking mood. I just wanted to know how to end this shit, so Ma's three season attire had to be pushed to the back of my mind. But with the way she kept catching my attention, I knew I was bound to crack on her ass soon.

"I'm glad you're all here! From the conversation I had with Lynx earlier, we're in for a fight. He didn't explain it all to me, but he did say that it was a lot of information to unpack. I want you all to brace yourselves for what's to come, but always know we act as a unit. Lynx takes full responsibility for what has happened, and before he steps into this room, I want y'all to know, I'm still backing him. Gabe, that's your son in-law, but I don't want you to feel like you must choose him or us. We're riding with him on this one, because I trust that he's gonna get this shit handled."

Hearing Ju speak about Lynx had me snapping back into our reality. That nigga had to be smoking that shit! "Who gon' be backing him? Speak for your damn self! You can ride with his ass 'cause ion wanna ride! We talking 'bout the Federales coming to our house and taking us from our families! Well, Ju, I mean it'll be good for you 'cause you gon' have all yo' lil gang bangin' ass kids with you! I'm sure if you asked, you could bunk with Zelan, and they will put Kari, Jah, JuJu, and Myah all next to you. Ohhh lawd, me and my daddy going to jail! Tru, I heard them heshem's (he/ She/Them) like to look at you and blink their eyes at you.

Ion wanna be a heshem! I like having Gia. Ion got time to be worrying about somebody trying to take my bootyhole, lawd! When they let us out for chow, I'ma have to put tape over my bootyhole just in case we got some aggressive niggas in there. Nahhhh, this shit ain't gon' work for me! Mmmmm mmmm! See, I came over here in hopes that you had a plan to get out this shit, but you talking about some damn backing Lynx? And what you mean, son in-law? Malayah ain't mine! That damn girl came out with a head just as big as them muthafuckas I built them contraptions for! That ain't no son in-law of mine!

I'm about to go back to the house and have Caroline lil' cousin teach me how to twirl my muthafuckin' neck in a circle 'cause put me in the insane asylum and rip me out the straight jacket! I'm acting brand new! I rather fight off these crazy niggas, than to be fighting off Jeromenisha!"

I was serious as hell! If they came for us, I'm pleading insanity. Take a look back in history! All them white serial killers played crazy and spent the rest of their days dressed in all white, getting high off medication, and eating Jell-O. Yeah, that was my future right there. As a matter of fact, let me stop telling they ass my plan before they copy it! All of our asses can't have the same damn plea. A few minutes later, Lynx and about ten of his crew members walked into the room.

"Lynx, Malik, Nori, it's good to see y'all. I hate it had to be on these conditions," Juelz greeted them.

"I hate this shit has happened. I know you all want to know what's going on, and I don't want to hold any information from you. JuJu, I just sent a video to your phone. Can you set it up on the screen for everyone to see it? I would rather y'all see what we working with first, and then I can speak after." Lynx looked over at JuJu, and I almost felt bad for the kid when I saw a glimmer of defeat in his eyes. I had to snap out of it thinking about them Heshems. I wondered if my contraptions could catch one of their asses? If the insanity role didn't work.

"Got it. Give me a few minutes to get up." Ju started working on his computer. A few minutes later, he turned the television on, and we couldn't believe what the fuck we were watching.

"Yo, who the fuck is this bitch! 'Cause ain't none of us going the fuck out like this. If this bitch wants, she gon' definitely get it. We're the wrong muthafuckin' family to come at with this shit! The fuck! Not only will we go down, but my muthafuckin' nieces and nephews too! Fuck that! This bitch gotta die, and that shit needs to happen today! Fuck tomorrow! All I want to see is her blood on the muthafuckin walls, and any other muthafucka that want it can get it!" Everything Zelan was spitting right now was the truth.

"You got that shit right! There has never been a bitch alive that could take this family down. We're GBC 'round this bitch, and we gon' be GBC until we die!" Ma's three seasons ass blurted.

"Ma, you and Pop got one leg in and the other leg out. Don't use that saying no mo', and the GBC members retired when yo' ass turned eighty," I told her.

"Nigga, I don't give a damn. I can be old as hell, but my team of shootas is always on go, and they stay ready!" I had to agree with her there. The guards on her squad would lay you down without breathing first to protect her ass.

"Who the fuck is she, and what does she want from all of this?" Juelz asked Lynx.

"Her name is Natalie Alvarez, and her father is Alonzo Alvarez! She was someone I used to sleep with. It was nothing more than that, but she wanted more, and now we're here. She also says that during our time together, she got pregnant, and she has a five-year-old daughter. All of this was before I reconnected with Malayah. Natalie wants me to leave my wife and marry her. She also wants me to sign my organization over to the Alvarez Cartel. That would include the percentages that I have with the Santiago Cartel," he explained.

"What! How does that even work? You're married to Layah. So, you're saying she wants you to leave Malayah?" Kari questioned in confusion.

"Yeah, and that's exactly what she wants him to do, and that's what his ass did! But I understand it 'cause I likes my damn freedom. I think yo' ass made a good ass choice! My baby heart broke now, but when she sues your ass for all of those millions she 'bout to get, her ass gon' be smiling all the way down to Ju bank with her check! And you and that crazy bitch can live happily ever after!

Hell, I can even cancel the date I had her set up with the head of the Manuel Cartel. Unless she runs through all that money. Then I'm putting her ass back on the dating scene. 'Cause I know this nigga didn't think he wasn't going to have to pay us some alimony, child support, and some mental support. He should ask Juelz ass all about that mental support he had to pay Ci back in the day from breaking her heart."

"What's going on?" Meek asked, walking into the room.

"Oh, nigga, now yo' ass wanna show up when all our asses 'bout to go to jail on four hundred counts of murder! You better get on your knees, do a praise break and thank gawd that you weren't with us. I'ma start hanging with you and Toya asses 'cause y'all don't ever be in our bullshit! You know, I'm starting to think your unfriendly ass plans it like that." I fanned his ass off. Zelan filled him in on everything, and he was on the same shit. It's time to strap up and give this bitch that work.

"I did break things off with my wife last night. You all can hate me for it, but I did it because I'll never allow my son to be without his mother or sit and watch my wife in jail. I may have made some decisions prematurely, but it was the first thing I could think of on such short notice. Every move I make, I do it not only to shield my family but to protect my organization. My brother and cousins only do what I ask of them. They don't deserve to go down for shit. I made my decision for not only them, but all of you. You all don't deserve any of this shit either, and I'll never let some bitch come in and think she's going to take you down. I know I may have hurt my wife, and I'm sorry as fuck for doing that to her. I had to make some quick decisions because Natalie is unstable, and I don't want her making moves that I don't know about.

I think the best option for all of us is if I'm in the house with her so that way I can keep an eye on her. This isn't a permanent situation; I'm coming back for my wife. I just don't know how long this will take. She has this video in the hands of other people, so if something happens to her, the video goes to the Feds. This shit is way bigger than Malayah, and our vows and I say that as respectfully as I can," Lynx exhaustedly stated.

The dude really did look stressed. I guess I could understand where he was coming from in this situation. There were too many people's lives at stake.

"Alonzo Alvarez has always been a snake in the grass, and with snakes, you have to cut their heads off. I'm here for whatever you need. I have plenty of resources, and they're all at your disposal," Pop Santiago told him.

"I've alerted the Diamond Clique, and they're gearing up to head to New York now." Kari stood to her feet, mad as fuck.

"Yeah, bro, we got you. Whatever you need, we're here. I appreciate the fuck outta you for what you're doing for all of us. This shit could've solely been about you saving yours, but you sacrificed your family to fix this shit. I'm forever grateful and ready to help you end this bitch, so you can get back to your wife and child." Jah stood to dap him up, and everyone else followed.

"Lynx, can you give me everything you have on this Natalie chick? I need her phone numbers, any known addresses, current and old, any friends you might know of, and the same for her parents. I need everything on them. The sooner I get that information, the sooner I can find out who she sent those videos too." JuJu was already on it.

"If Bill Gates is on the case, and the muthafuckin' Diamond Clique is on the way. Yessuuhhhh, we 'bout to have a time! Eeeewwwweeeee! We 'bout to have a muthafuckin' time! Kari and the clique 'bout to kill everything moving in that damn house! Wheeewwww! I need me a damn blunt! I'm alright though. We're all going to be alright.

Don't let this hoe rattle y'all one bit, even though this shit is bad. We got this, and we gon' get her ass, just as sure as my name is Laila Santiago!" Ma pulled out her blunt, lit it, and my ass was right beside her because I needed to be real high to let this shit go. I'm with her. If we start moving like we nervous, this crazy bitch gon' think she got us where she wants us. We all sat around and chopped it up, trying to come up with a plan to take this bitch out. And from the looks of things, I think we got this shit under control.

CHAPTER 7

Lynx

I'm glad things went well with Malayah's family. My father in-law even pulled me to the side and told me he was with me. That was big coming from his crazy ass, and I truly appreciated it. I'm glad they understood where I was coming from regarding my wife. I'm hoping that Malayah can understand it all. Being with her parents is the best thing for her right now because that leaves me free to take care of Natalie. The way I'm feeling right now, I could lay down this entire fuckin' city.

I can't lie like my life taking a drastic turn didn't have a nigga out here feeling lost. The nagging feeling of my wife not wanting me back was in the rear of my mind, and refused to be stilled. Rolling over in bed without her warm, soft body in reach for me to scoop up and place on my dick had me out here feeling like I was about to go into cardiac arrest. I know Layah was feeling like I had given up on her, but that shit was the furthest thing from the truth. Decisions that hurt you and the people you love must be made when you're the boss, and I wouldn't be the boss if I didn't make them.

I can't believe I let this bitch come in and shake shit up in my damn organization. Never in life have I ever allowed a nigga, let alone some wannabe boss ass bitch, to come in and do that shit to me. The decisions I make are always calculated with a plan, and for now, the decision to separate from my wife is best for all of us. Natalie is a piece of fuckin' work. I know her and the best part about all of this shit is I know how she operates. This shit isn't about marrying me. That bitch wants all of the power she knows she can have by bridging both of our organizations. If she did, that makes her a very powerful woman.

The best place for me is on the inside with her to watch her moves, but best believe I'm killing all these muthafuckas. I got us into the shit, and I'm going to be the one to get us out of it. One thing I did a couple of years ago was put that lil' smart ass JuJu on my payroll and contracted Jah. That was the best move I could've ever made because it makes our moves so much easier. Pulling out my phone, I dialed the number and waited for this pussy muthafucka to answer.

"I've been expecting your call." Alonzo's voice vibrated through the speaker.

"Do you know what you've created by allowing her to do this shit!" I was mad as fuck because this muthafucka sounded as if he was amused by all of this.

"Lynx, you know how my daughter is. She always gets what

she wants, and she wants it all. You should have thought about your decision to cut ties with us. It was at a time when I needed you the most. We were at war, and you turned your back on us. Not to mention you hurt my daughter's feelings. She had your daughter, and you decided to house another bitch!" he chuckled.

I let out a breath to calm down. "I'll see you real soon." I ended the call because there wasn't shit else, I needed to say to his ass. Looking over at Nori and Malik I just shook my head.

"What's your next move?" Nori asked.

"Making sure we find these videos and get them all deleted or in our possession and ensuring that all of the people she sent it to are dead." I stood from my seat. We were all staying at Aunt Nadine's house, and that made me think of something.

"Bruh, why are you staying here? Everything cool with you and Tasha?" Looking over at him, I see that mentioning her name is pissing him off.

"What's up with this nigga?" Malik asked, noticing the change in Nori.

"With everything that's going on, I didn't even want to bring this shit up, but since you niggas asked, here it is." Nori pinched the bridge of his nose.

"Tasha thought I was away on an assignment, and I came home early to surprise her. I was gonna take her on a lil' trip to Jamaica because I had been gone a lot in the past couple of months. I felt like my girl deserved some special attention from her man. When I got inside the house, I could hear music playing, but I didn't think anything of it until I looked at the dining room table; it was a place setting for two. They had steak and wine from what I could see, so I started paying close attention to the music that was playing and the clothes that was spread all of over my staircase-"

"Nigga, I know you not gon' say what I think you gon' say! Tasha?!" Malik cut him off, but I was feeling the same damn way. Tasha has always been that down ass chick for Nori. We ran the damn blocks together; Tasha was our runner when we needed her back in the day. She loved that nigga dirty drawers, so I couldn't even fathom what this nigga was about to say.

"She had another nigga in my bed, fucking that nigga." He glanced past us as if he was staring into space. The worry lines etched in his forehead told me the answers to my next question, but fuck it, I needed to ask that shit.

"Which part of the country did you send his body parts?" I questioned.

"Inferno."

"And Tasha?" Malik and I both were so invested that we asked the question at the same damn time.

"She's still breathing, but it's taking everything in me not to end her daily. I go over to the house every day with the intention of blowing that bitch's head off. I hate a disloyal mutha-fucka, and Tasha is one disloyal bitch! I gave that girl everything. This is what she does to me! Man, fuck that hoe with an Aids infected dick!"

"Damn, nigga, you mad. I understand why you didn't do her, but you of all people know we don't leave anything or anybody to chance. Look at what the fuck we got going on right now, and that's a mess that I have to clean the fuck up. I'm sorry, bro, but you know that Tasha has to go to sleep. I feel fucked up about it because we grew up with her ass, but I don't see any other way to handle this shit. This isn't about us, but you really don't know how she felt about ole boy. That shit could have been deep, but something she couldn't tell you. Make it look an accident so her family can give her a proper burial. I gotta go. It's time for me to check in on my wife and get back to Puerto Rico. We will be heading to Mexico to Mexico tomorrow. Oh, and another thing, I'm need y'all to close all operations until this shit is done. I don't want shit moving because who know, this bitch might have already leaked us to the feds. I got somebody on the inside looking into any open cases regarding us or the Kassom organization. Hit me up if y'all need me." I gave them both a brotherly hug and went to say my goodbyes to Aunt Nadine and Bria. I hope Nori understood where we were coming from regarding Tasha. And I damn sure hoped Malik worked things out with Bria because I knew they loved each other.

Twenty minutes later, my driver pulled up to the security gates at Malayah's parents' house. He pulled up close enough for the retina scan to read my eyes, and the gates opened. I was surprised that Gabe granted me that type of access, he said he was tired of them calling every time I brought my ass over. When we pulled up to the house, my father in-law was outside trimming one of his trees.

"Sup, Pop!" I spoke, getting out of the truck.

"Nigga, I'm not yo' Pop 'til you come back and get these

homeless people outta my house. I asked yo' ass was you still rich, but the real question I should've been asking you was yo' ass free of any crazy bitches! How you get hooked up with that chick? Never mind, don't answer that JuJu showed us a picture, and she finer than a muthafucka, so I see how. But her crazy shoulda overpowered you trying to get some pussy. Let me know if you need me to do anything. I know you in a hell of a situation." He patted me on my back and went back to trimming his tree, and I headed inside the house. Malayah was in the kitchen on the phone, and when she saw me, she ended the call.

"Why are you here? Shouldn't you be with her?" she rolled her eyes, and turned away.

Normally I had all the patience in the world with my wife, but I was operating on a short fuse. "You gotta stop talking to me like that. You know I don't do that disrespect shit at all with you or anybody else that deals with me. Yes, I could've done shit differently, but for the hundredth time, this girl has proof of us committing several murders, and you and your family are all up in that shit. What will our son do if both of his parents are locked the fuck up, Layah? Huh? You a fucking lawyer, ma! Think! You have to understand where I'm coming from and the position I'm taking in this situation. Are you really thinking about that shit? Or are you in yo' feelings because you can't get your fuckin' way? I'm going to get to the bottom of this, find out who has the videos, and resolve the issue. You're here, and this is the best place for you and Bray right now," I explained as calmly as I could.

"Whatever, Lynx! I'm through with the situation. My

biggest problem is that without a second thought, you jumped in headfirst and never considered me! You never considered talking to me and us maybe coming up with a plan together. I fully understand helping all of us get out of this situation, but I'm still a wife! Your fucking wife! My feelings should always come before anything and anyone else. It's called respect! If you want it, you have to give it, and that's always been my policy.

Send me the video that everyone is talking about, and I'll start to do my own investigation. I'm here to help in any way that I can because my family needs me, and Bray needs his father, but I'm filing for a divorce. I can't do this shit with you right now.

It seems when shit gets hot you feel like you're on your own, and I'm not with that shit at all. My feelings are hurt, and you're so ready to jump into Cartel action that you don't care about that. I'm not going to sit around knowing you're sharing time, space, and a bed with another woman. This is the reason I ran from niggas like you in the first place! I never wanted to go through this shit. I know there is someone out there that's not in this profession that will love me, and care for me the way that I need to be cared for" She turned to walk away, and that shit set me the fuck off, causing me to snatch her ass right the fuck up.

"Don't fuck with me! You know why I'm doing this, and you know who your husband is! Don't get a nigga killed over emotions. Some things are hard as fuck to do, but when it comes to my family, I will walk on burning coals to get to any bitch that's fuckin' with mine! This is your only warning! If I see or find out that you're entertaining any nigga in anything other than a professional relationship, I'ma dead that nigga just as sure as my name is Lynx Carter. Don't make these mothers have to bury their sons, 'cause your emotional ass is out here throwing temper tantrums!

I've only shown you the side of me that loves you and my child. You haven't met this side of me, and I promise you neither one of us wants that muthafucka to come out, especially not with you. This version of me thinks different, acts different, and fucks different, and we BOTH know you can't handle that shit. Don't play those types of games with me; nothing about my ass is stable. You may think this bitch is running the show, but she's giving me time to calculate my thoughts, and that move was the wrong move!" I gritted, pulling her closer to me. Gabe came running in the house screaming like fire was attached to his ass.

"Ahhh, helllll nawl! Giaaaa, that crazy bitch is out there! This bitch sliding her gun back and forth on my iron gate like them women be in them Fatal Attraction movies. That bitch out there talkin, *'bout heyyy, Gabeeee*! I said noooo, bitch! My name Chester; Gabeeee the fuck moved last night! What that bitch got a Lo-jack on ya dick or summin'? Ohhhh, lawd! This bitch could come while we sleep and stand over me thinking my sexy ass is you!" He started pacing back and forth, and the way this nigga was acting I had to chuckle, but I could see the concern on my mother in-law and wife's face.

"I got this; everything will be alright. I'll keep her away from here, I promise." I didn't want them to think that I would allow her to bring this to their doorstep or hurt them.

THE CARTER CARTEL: LYNX CARTER

"Lynx, be careful out there. Don't worry, we got her and Brayden. Thank you for trying to protect our family from this crazy bitch! Trust me, I'm ready to go out there and beat her ass-"

Gabe interrupted her. "And I'm not coming to get yo' ass, Gia. One thing Gabe don't mess with, and that's crazy and a crazy bitch with Fatal Attraction tendencies. Gon', nigga, get her ass and take y'all problems back to Puerto Rico or Mexico, wherever the hell she from!" I was pissed the fuck off that this bitch would even come here. He's right though. How did her ass know that I was here? I ran upstairs to see my son.

"Papppiiii!" He ran to jump into my arms.

"Hey, kiddo. I can't stay but know that Papi loves you with everything in me. I'll be back to get you and mommy soon, okay? Use your iPad to call me as much as you want. You remember how to call me, right?"

"Yes, Papi. I luh you." Bray was such a smart little boy. He was so advanced with everything, and I was so proud of my lil guy. His mom felt like we should get him into early learning, and that helped his development a lot. I wasn't always home with him, but when I was, I felt the need to teach my son the importance of knowing that he'd always have me in his life. When I was kid, I didn't have that, and I made a promise to never be that type of nigga. Which is why doing what I have to do is so important to me. My son needs his mother and father with him. If my wife can't understand that, then I guess she'll never get it. I said my goodbyes to my son and everyone else and headed outside. Natalie was indeed fuckin' crazy because this bitch and her security were definitely out here like she was the fuck right.

"What the fuck are you doing? You gave me three days, and that shit ain't up yet. I have to make sure that my wife and kid are alright!" I roared, walking up on her.

"I hope you made that shit worth it because this is the last time, you're going to see them. After tonight, we're going to be married and raising our own family. I have a judge that's going to finalize your divorce and rush it through. The documents of your signing over your organization have already been drawn up, and I'm here because I want to fly to Mexico with my man. Awwww, look. Your little bitch came out to say goodbye, give me a kiss and let's give her something to see." I turned, and Malayah was standing outside watching us.

"Give me a fucking kiss!" She demanded, and regret washed all over me. I hated that I had to play along with this girl, but if I wanted to get what I needed, I had to do it. Leaning in, I gave her a kiss, and that shit hurt me more than it did my wife. Looking in her direction and seeing the pain in her eyes damn near killed me. I sent Ju a text letting him know it was a change in plans and for him to leave and head straight to Mexico. Once I hit send and saw that he read it, my whole phone shut down, and everything that I had in my phone was deleted. It was as if I had just gone in the store and purchased a new damn phone. I had to smile because I knew it was Ju that just deleted my shit. That lil' nigga was smart as fuck.

CHAPTER 8

Malayah

Being back in New York makes me feel good, because that means I'm with my family. I was hurt by this entire situation, and I just couldn't see past that pain. The whole world seemed to be moving in slow motion. I felt like I was walking in a dream world. A horrific, nightmarish dream world. I thought maybe seeing Lynx and us talking would fix things, but my anger towards him only heightened. My heart shattered the entire time he was in my presence, and there was this falling, spinning down feeling. I was so messed up seeing him kiss that girl that that shit had me ready to take my gun and open fire on both their asses. When I love, I love hard, and my husband, in my eyes, was everything to me. I felt like my heart was being ripped from my body. All of this shit just happened over night, and I can't get past it.

Trust me, I get it, but I have the right to feel the way I do. I can't just sit back and watch him be with another woman. Call me weak, call me selfish, call me what the fuck you want; I'm not built like that. I know it's levels to this street shit, and I gotta have tough skin, but nah, fuck that, I can't rock with that. I'm so glad Melani came over, and we were able to spend some time together. I didn't realize it, but I needed my big sister and the love that only a sister could give was needed. I had plans to go over and see her and Mano tonight.

"Are you alright, boo?" Bri asked, sitting next to me at the kitchen table. I went to visit her over at Aunt Nadine's house. I'm never really here without my husband, and it felt so damn weird. I couldn't help but to keep turning my head toward the door, praying he'd walk through it, but I knew he was with that bitch. Just thinking about them fucking had me swallowing back vomit.

"Sup? What y'all got going on?" Romel asked as he took the food out of the fridge to warm up. Mel, Nori's older brother, worked closely with the guys in the organization. He was such a cool cousin, and me and Bri loved his ass. We always called him twin because he looked so much like Lynx you would think they were brothers versus Nori.

"Nothing just sitting here trying to cheer her up," Bri sang, and I gave him a half smile.

"Yeah, cheer that shit right on up, because we gon' put that bitch in the dirt where she belongs. It ain't never a good thing fuckin' with us. I don't give a fuck who you are or how powerful you think you are. Big cuz gone always come out on top, and that's on me! Just don't give up on my cuz. One thing I know for certain, that nigga love you, and he got this shit in the bag." He kissed the top of my head, grabbed his food, and headed out of the kitchen.

"Love Mel. He always knows what to say to make things better." Bri stood from her seat to go get some of the food he took out the fridge and didn't put the hell back. Aunt Nadine would have kicked his ass, but I'm with Bri. I wanted some of that shit too, because it smelled so damn good.

"Fix me a plate, sis." I smiled, and she fanned me off.

"I shouldn't fix your apple head ass nothing. You always wait for me to get up to do something and then ask me to fix your shit." She laughed. Once she heated the food up, we sat and ate. Lawd, Aunt Nadine put her whole foot in this food! I swear that lady needs to open a soul food spot, and I'll help her do it if she wants to.

"Have you figured out your situation with Malik?" I asked her.

"No, I feel like I'm just existing there. I know I need to let him know how I feel and what's really going on with me, but how do you tell a man that loves you, and don't get me wrong I love him too. But how do I tell him that I blame him for our daughter's death? I mean, I know that would hurt him, and I'm just not ready for that type of energy. I know what that would do to him, and I know that I would go into defense mode. I truly don't know what to do about it. Sometimes I think I should just push through like I have for the last few years." She shrugged, and seeing Malik standing in the doorway behind us damn near knocked the wind out of me. I tried my best to nod at Bri and alert her, but I felt paralyzed.

"So, you fuckin' blame me for our daughter's death! The hell that I've put on my mental that night, and the days, months, and years trying to figure out how I could make you better. While I sat in misery over losing my baby girl and all this time you blamed me for her death! Bii-" He stopped himself because he was truly losing it.

"Malik, baby...I'm so sorry, I've been trying to find ways to talk to you about it, but I just couldn't find the words to tell you. I didn't want it to be like this. I just feel like if we weren't playing in the car, you would've been paying better attention to the road, and the accident wouldn't have happened!" Bri cried as she tried to walk up to him and grab his hand, but he snatched it back.

"Get the fuck off me! You were the one that started playing in the car! If you didn't grab my dick, we wouldn't have started playing in the car. The fuck is you talking about! Don't try to put all of this on me! It was an accident, and in some ways, yes, I could have done more! And yes, I blame myself because, as a man, I'ma always take the burden on my back! I never wanted this shit to happen to us. I would give my own fuckin' life and lay down right now to have our daughter with us! This shit has been killing me inside, and now you come with this shit! Fuck you, Bria!" He stormed out of the kitchen, and she tried her best to run after him.

My heart was in shambles for her because I knew they loved each other, and that shit hurt him because he was shedding tears while talking to her.

"What is going on?" Aunt Nadine came down the stairs, and Nori and Mel were right behind her.

"This chick blames me for our baby dying! Listen, I love you, ma, but I'm going back to Puerto Rico. I'll see you soon." He kissed his aunt and walked out the door.

"Ohhh, dear God." Aunt Nadine pulled Bria into her arms and started praying for all of us. Bria cried so hard her body shook. I stayed until she calmed down enough to go upstairs to take a nap. She said she didn't plan on going back to Puerto Rico until tomorrow, hoping that it would give Malik time to calm down. It seemed as if everything revolving around the Carter men was a disaster, and it worried the hell out of Aunt Nadine. I left and headed back to my parent's house because going through the emotions of Bri and Malik's issues made me sad.

"Zayah, all I want is my divorce, and I want it done quickly. I know you can make that happen, friend. You're the best divorce attorney in the land," I joked.

"Who gon' tell you, you're wrong when you're right? The Best! You hear me!" We both fell out laughing.

"I just think you might be moving too fast, friend, but I'm not going to get in your way. Are we asking for anything from the marital estate?" She asked, but I didn't need anything from Lynx.

"Nope, I got me and Bray." Before I knew it, my phone was being snatched out of my hand.

"Hol up...hold thee hell up! Don't listen to her ass! That nigga is a billionaire! He got plenty of money we can get. I'm tired of her free-loading ass thinking she can come here and eat up all my damn butter pecan ice cream and Pecan Sandy cookies. Every time I want a snack, ion got no mo' 'cause her lil' fish mouth ass and her Step Into The Light ass son done ate my shit. Mmmm, mmmmm, we bouts to go for the gusto, and if he says no, we taking his Big Lip The Rock lookin' ass to court!

If he worth a billion, we want nine hundred and ninety-nine milli in our bank account by morning. Hell wrong with you! You just gon' let his ass take all the money for Cruella to have? Hell nawl! We ain't giving shit but space in our bank account to collect all his muthafuckin' change. Za- Za, you need his phone number?" My dad asked Zayah, and her ass was too busy laughing at his ass.

"No, I have it, Mr. Gabe. I miss you and Ms. Gia. Can't wait to see you again," she expressed to my dad, and his ass was smiling hard.

"We miss you too, my spades partner. This girl mentioned to me this morning that she wanted to go on vacation to Belize soon. Hopefully, you can join us." My dad loved my friends, and they absolutely adored him and my mom. All my friends loved it when I was home, just so they can laugh and joke with my damn dad. I didn't want to sit and soak in my misery, so I decided to pack a bag and go hang out with my sister. I refused any of Lynx's security detail the moment I got back into New York, and I'm driving my old car that had shipped from Cali. My dad felt like I shouldn't have stopped the security, but I wanted nothing from him right now. Even though I gave it up, I just couldn't shake the feeling that someone was following me.

CHAPTER 9
Malik

I couldn't believe the shit I overheard. And the fact that her ass was sitting around all these damn years, not trying to heal. I begged this woman to let's go get some help. Even if we did that shit separately. I love the fuck out of that woman, and I just can't believe we let our shit get like this. I'll never forget the night I met her beautiful ass and things changed for us.

"Damn, you giving them shorts hell, baby girl."

"Umm...Hey."

"What you doing out in the hall showing off my shit?" I said to her, and she started looking around as if I was speaking to somebody else.

"Excuse me, this belongs to me. I'm just looking for my friend because she was supposed to bring me some food from downstairs. I guess she forgot about me." She shrugged.

"Nah, she's down in the lobby talking to my brother. But come on, lil baby. You can eat with me."

"Noo, that's ok. I don't wanna impose on you when you're trying to eat your dinner and relax," she told him.

"Let's go, lil baby. The first thing to learn about me is I hate repeating myself. We 'bout to go bust this shit down and get to know one another, witcho pretty ass." I smiled at her.

I've loved that girl from that day on, and I only wanted to make her days on this earth the best days of her life. Bria had my heart, and I would've given her the world, hell I laid that shit at her feet. When she first called off the wedding, her excuse was she had to get her mind right. After a year had passed by, I asked her again, but she still wasn't ready. So I said that I wouldn't pressure her. We were actively trying to have another baby. She wanted that, and if that's what she wanted, that's what I would give her. But she hasn't gotten pregnant, and now I overhear this shit. Her ass probably been feeling this way since the day we had the accident.

I'm so fuckin' mad I could tear this fuckin' house apart right now. The way I'm feeling scared the shit out of me for many reasons. If she felt that way about me, I'm ready to let her ass walk. This was hard as fuck because I loved this girl, and to think of not having her fucked me up. I've always said this about Bri, she doesn't know how to heal. She keeps things so bottled up inside and holds on for so long that she lets things fester until they combust. Now our shit might be at the end of the road because she wasn't woman enough to come sit down and talk to me. I would have been upset, but I would have respected her feelings a little better if it was me that she talked to instead of Layah.

I'm not fighting for this shit with her a day longer. I fought like a muthafucka trying to nurse my girl back from this tragic moment. Not one time did she care about how I was feeling. Not one time did she come wrap her arms around me and tell me she had me and that everything would be alright. Not one muthafuckin' time! The fuck is wrong with this girl!

My phone ringing phone jolted me out of my thoughts. I wasn't going to answer it until I saw my brother's name and immediately picked up.

"Sup, you good? I just got a call from Nori. I'm sorry that shit happened to you, bro. We got this shit here; I need you to take a step back and get your mental together. I know that shit fucked you up, because it fucked me up to hear that. If you love her, fight for her. We both know she's been fighting this shit for a long time, and I know you have too, but she's the one that carried that child and felt her baby move every day.

We may say that she should've gotten over it by now, but we can't say that shit. Everybody is different. Think about that before you make a rash decision that could change shit for y'all forever. I know you, and I know how you operate. You will call this shit quits in a heartbeat; remember you asked this woman to be your wife." I understood where my brother was coming from, but I'm not trying to hear that shit right now.

"I hear you. What's up with you? I'm not taking any breaks until we get you out of there and everyone is cleared." And I meant that shit. We had to get to the bottom of this shit and quick. I'm ready to pop every family member that bitch got down to the muthafuckin' cat and dog, fuck it. Anybody that bitch consider family, I consider the fuck dead.

"I'm not using my regular phone. I' ma stay on this burner, so call me on here. JuJu is blocking any taps and erasing any history on this phone. Get Ju on the call with us." I clicked over and dialed Ju up. That dude is a fuckin' mastermind, and we been needed him on our time. I for sure damn sure appreciate Juelz for suggesting he come on payroll.

"What's up, M?" He picked up on the first ring.

"I got Lynx on the call with us." I placed the call on speaker.

"L, what's up?" Ju questioned.

"Sup. Do you have any information on who she's been talking to? Any family members we should know about?" Lynx was on the same damn page I was on.

"Yeah, I got something interesting that me and my sister in-law Remi found. There are two calls that she made right before she approached you in the restaurant. Remi is in the process of doing a sweep of their information now," he informed him, and you could hear his damn fingers tearing that damn keyboard up.

"We gon' keep shit on the low, but that bitch time is coming to an end, and it's coming real soon. I don't like leaving shit lingering around too long. Malik, if you're not taking a break, I need for y'all to get everything you can on this bitch. I want everybody close to this family looked at."

"I got you." I'm glad my brother called because this conversation definitely got my attention off home shit.

"Lynx, did you ever look at your security detail that was with you in New York during the times of those deaths?? I finished my evaluations on their personal phones and computers. I didn't get anything from them, but that doesn't mean anything," he said to Lynx.

"They're dead; I'm leaving nothing to chance. Some of those men have been with me from the beginning, and if they didn't have anything to do with it, oh well. This comes with the territory. My security is a unit, and as a unit, you ride together, you die together. I'm going to kill everybody in my camp until I get to the right nigga. I gotta go. Just let me know what you find on this bitch family and friends. Brief Malik and Nori on it, if you can't get me on the phone. Bro, call this line if you need me. Remember what I said about the home front." He ended the call.

"Ju, let me know if you need me for anything."

"Will do." We spoke for a few more minutes and ended the call. I heard the doors chime and took a deep breath because I knew it was Bria. I was hoping that she would stay longer. Nori punk ass was supposed to text me and let me know when she left. I sipped the drink I was nursing as I heard her entering the room.

"Malik, can we please talk? I just need you to hear me out. I kept my feelings from you because I didn't want to hurt you. There was no way that I could do that, I wouldn't be able to face you after that, and some days I go back and forth with it. Trust me, I blamed myself as well, but she was my baby girl! I wanted our daughter to survive! I wanted my baby so bad! Please understand how bad I'm hurting over this.

Maybe I'm wrong for having those thoughts, but I don't know what else to do. I've tried to push them to the back of my head, baby. I don't want to have any type of resentment when it comes to you. I love you! I just want my baby! I can't do anything else but think of her. It was the moment the first pain hit me; I could literally feel the air leaving my body. Do you know how bad I felt? I was empty inside." She stood in the doorway crying, and I swear I felt nothing right now. Normally, when she cries, I'm quick to pull her into my arms and let her get everything she needed to get out.

I sat there for a minute reflecting on our relationship. "I would say I don't know where shit went bad with us, but I guess I do know. It went bad the night of the accident, the night it was so-called my fault! The night you believe I killed our fuckin' daughter! The night the love fuckin' disappeared! The fuck! If you blame me for that shit, stand ten fuckin' toes down on yo' shit, lil baby! Don't come in this bitch talking 'bout sometimes I feel that way and sometimes I don't! Nah, when you were talking to Layah at Ma house, it was I blame that nigga! I remember every fuckin' word. Let me help you remember that shit!

No, I feel like I'm just existing with him. I know I need to let him know how I feel and what's really going on with me.

Does that shit sound familiar yet?!

How do you tell a man that loves you that I BLAME him for

our daughter's death! Like I said, stand on that muthafucka, Bria!

I mean, I know that would hurt him, and I'm just not ready for that type of energy. I know what that would do to him.

Oh, you gon' get all this energy, and you can clearly see what it's doing to me! I did my best to be the man you needed. I've never thought about cheating on you, even when there were months where you rejected me. I've given you love, affection and provided you with the best life. I even talked to you about us going to get help, and you rejected that shit too.

Everything that a man should be in your life, I've given you that shit, and I'ma always stand on that shit! You can walk away today or tomorrow, and you can't tell the next muthafucka shit about Malik Carter and how he treated and took care of you 'cause I'm that nigga! I need you to stay the fuck away from me for a lil' minute. Go figure out if this some shit you wanna rock out with me in and get back to me. You cut my back out with this fuck shit here, and don't get me wrong I think about my child daily! I was fighting so many of my own battles about you losing her. Hell, I blamed myself for not paying closer attention. But damn, shorty, that's what the fuck you on?" I was mad as fuck, so I jumped out of bed and rushed past her. She stood hysterically crying, but I couldn't deal with her ass right now. Nor did I want to.

CHAPTER 10
Bria

I was sitting here listening to *Life and Favor by John P. Kee & New Life.* It's a song that I used to love listening to with my grandmom, and anytime I felt like I was going through a storm. I couldn't stop the tears from falling. I was devastated knowing that Malik had overheard my conversation with Malayah. Life has been so hard for me that, at times, I could barely pull myself out of bed. I tried seeking help on my own, but the pain was just so grave for me. People may not understand how I feel until you've gone through this as a mother.

I don't think they could tell me everything is going to be ok or give me advice. That may be selfish to say, but that's how I feel. My daughter was a human being. Her little organs were developed and only getting stronger so that she could be born. She was a part of me. She moved uncontrollably inside of me at times, and every time she did it, I cried. I always figured she was playing around and trying to interact with her mommy. Being pregnant was everything to me. It was an amazing feeling, and I was so in love with knowing that my child would soon be born.

For weeks after my miscarriage, I tried to fight off my thoughts and feelings. Before all of this happened, I was so in love with my man, and the day of my baby shower, when that man got on one knee, I felt like God allowed the sun to shine bright over my life. I have been living in hell, and it's true Malik has been there for me in ways that I couldn't imagine. He has cared for me, tried to get us counseling, held me as I cried, and taken me on trips just to get my mind off all that we were going through. The thing is, with all that he has done, my anger and finding his fault in the death of our daughter grew stronger. And even though I felt that way, I still loved him. I wanted to talk to him in hopes that he would understand how I was feeling, but he wanted nothing to do with me.

It's been a few days, and he hasn't said a word to me. The one time I tried to touch him, he snatched away in a rage, sending his fist into the wall. He was so angry with me, and I didn't know how to get through to him. I knew he wasn't going to hurt me, so I wasn't scared of him. I decided to call Lynx and talk to him because he's the only one that can get through to him.

"Yeah." Lynx raspy voice came through the receiver when he answered.

"Hey, Lynx. Do you have time to talk?" I asked him.

"Sup, Bri?"

"Lynx, I'm sure Malik has talked to you about what's going on with us. I don't know how to get through to him. I just need him to understand how I'm feeling about this and my reasoning for feeling the way that I do!" I cried.

"Baby girl, do you seriously think that he wants to hear what you have to say if you're going to continue to fault him? Like, did you even take the time to hear him grieve and go through his processes of loss? He had to do that shit with me, baby girl. That man loves you unconditionally and would go to the ends of the world to make sure you're good. Don't do him like that. It was an accident, and it was something I wished wouldn't have happened. That was my niece, and I grieved over her loss as well. We'll never forget her, Bri, but you have to start releasing that pain, baby.

If you feel that you can't let go of that blame, then you really don't need to be with my brother. That shit isn't good for you or him. I would love to see you flourish together, start your family, get married, and all that good shit. But it's time to heal, release, and let go. And that let go could end up in many different ways. I'm praying for your healing; I'm praying for you and my brother to heal together.

Think about what I've said, and whatever decisions you make, remember you gotta stand on that shit and live with it. Love you, baby girl." Hearing him out only made my thoughts more confused and crazier, but I understood him.

"Thank you for this talk. I love you too." We spoke for a few more minutes and then ended the call. I went into the bathroom to clean my face and headed downstairs to cook dinner.

Hearing Lynx mention starting a family made me think about my decision not to have another baby with Malik. I truly don't know why I've stayed with him this long. I think I'm just so scared to walk away from him because I still love him. It's just crazy to me. One minute, I hate him, and the next, I love him. I get thoughts of leaving him, but then I get thoughts of him being with someone else, falling in love, marrying her, and them having kids.

He walked into the kitchen and stared at me for a moment, then grabbed an energy drink from the fridge and walked right out. I rushed out of the kitchen and walked behind him.

"Malik, please talk to me! How much longer are we going to keep doing this!" I cried. He rushed over to me, penning me against the wall.

"Doing what?! Huh! What are we doing exactly?! The next time you open your mouth, I need to hear you say we're going to work through this together. We're going to get counseling; and move forward as a family unit. If you can't come to me with any of that, then you got some decisions to figure out, lil mama. When you do make them, please let me know because I need to start my healing from losing you and my daughter. I can't be right for the woman that God created for me if I'm not properly healed." The look in his eyes scared me. I have never seen that type of darkness in him before.

He turned and walked away. His words cut me deep. My stomach began churning with anxiety and frustration. I fell to my knees and just cried. I'm not sure where things will go from here with us.

CHAPTER 11
Natalie

Two Weeks Later

I have been getting a kick out of watching these muthafuckas suffer and go back and forth with this little bombshell I dropped on them. Lynx looked as if he was ready to tear some shit up, and I didn't give one fuck about his feelings. I loved that nigga down, and he did give a fuck about my feelings. Our last night together, I tried to open up and tell him about my feelings, but he straight up told me he wasn't into relationships. That he didn't ever think he was getting married. Yet he has this bitch he decided to give his last name to? I had to find a way to pay this nigga back.

We were in Mexico staying at the Alvarez compound, and I was happy as fuck that he was here with me. I just couldn't get the nigga to fuck me. I tried everything, but he's not giving in.

It pissed me off that he was in his feelings about being here with me and wanting to be with that bitch. I've thought about just ending her life. Then he wouldn't have any other choice but to move on. And the more I think about that shit, the more I think I should do that shit. I have some people keeping an eye on her, so I can pull the trigger anytime.

Now that I think about it, I can use that shit to my advantage. I love it when a plan comes together. Taking another pull from my blunt, I walked into the bedroom where Lynx was sleeping, as he ended his call.

"I thought you would like some company tonight." I crawled into bed with him, and he gripped me up by my neck so fast I barely could blink, pinning me against the wall.

"If you touch me again, I'ma forget what you have on me and kill your trifling ass!" He spat.

"I'm going to enjoy every moment of killing your bitch, and since you want to be stingy with the dick, I'm going to let you watch her die. I was going to leave her out of this and let you save them from these charges, but I think it's best that she's out of the way!" I laughed, and his ass looked as if he was ready to fuck me up.

"If you touch my muthafuckin' wife, bitch! I'm killing you and every nigga on this compound, and I promise you nothing will save you! You got to be a desperate bitch to try and fuckin' threaten a nigga to fuck you. Bitch, I'll go in the pasture out back and fuck one of them donkey's before I stick dick in you." When he tightened his grip, I'm not going to lie, I was a little shaken by his threat, but I would never let him see me sweat.

THE CARTER CARTEL: LYNX CARTER

"I'm going back to Puerto Rico tomorrow; I still have a business to run, and I don't have time to sit here with your crazy ass every day. When I get back, I need my so-called daughter here so we can get that DNA test going. How the fuck you got time to watch me day in and day out, but I haven't seen said child once since I've been here? Hoe, you unfit!" He left the room.

I was trying my best not to snap off on this nigga, but he was definitely trying my patience. My daughter was good and well taken care of, and even though he was screaming that DNA shit, it would happen on my time and my terms.

"Natalie, please come down." My father's voice echoed through the intercom. Walking out of the bedroom and heading over to the North side of the compound where my parents lived, I got excited with every step I took because I knew what was happening. My mother filled me in earlier, and she was just as excited as I was. Once I made it into their living quarters, they were in the family room talking.

"Natalie, here are the documents. You are now the head of the Alvarez Cartel. I'm so proud of you for all that you've done for this family. I don't want your new position to start off in a war. I want you to really think about what you're doing. There's only one reason Lynx Carter is here, and trust me, it's for his own reasons. Not because you think you have something over him. You've played your hand; now he knows what you're holding.

I've studied Lynx for years, and his steps are calculated. Everything that you've heard about him is true. He could look you in your eyes lovingly and could be having your mother killed while doing so. One thing I know about Lynx is that he's already working to take us down, and that goes for the Kassom family as well. Juelz Kassom is a mastermind right along with Lynx Carter.

The two of them together will cause mass destruction, and there isn't a damn thing we would be able to do about it. I've done a little more homework on Juelz, and it's something I don't think you've looked into regarding him, and that's his children and who they're married too. You see Kari Kass-" I cut his ass off because I don't give a fuck about Juelz, his children, or this bitch Kari.

My father has always been a fool when it comes to his business. He's trusted too many people and has always gotten the short end of the stick. He cared too much about connecting with the other organizations instead of making these muthafuckas lie down. It's true we're broke, and me nor my mother wanted to be out here working or begging muthafuckas to help us.

"Alonzo, it's because of her that we're here now. You should have turned everything over to her before now. You have always been a soft nigga! Never having a backbone and standing up to these people! Because of her quick thinking, we won't lose our home! We can live a comfortable life again! We now have money to pay our staff. It was hard as hell faking it like we had it and we didn't have shit!" My mother yelled in his face as she stood from the table, and he looked at her as if she was crazy.

"Do you know who you're speaking to like that?! Sit your ass down, Carmen!" He jumped up and grabbed my mother.

"No, it's time for you to lay down, Papa! You've always been weak as hell, you let us talk you right out of your operation. Pussy ass, it's always been me and Ma never you, bitch!" I pulled my gun out and let off two shots to his chest.

"Fuck! Ma, help me get him to the basement. I'll have him moved later tonight. Let's move him just in case Lynx heard the shots."

"You didn't say you were going to kill him right away! Fuck! You should've waited until we made sure everything on the document was legit! Make sure you get Felix to move his body. He'll know what to do and will do anything for me anyway." She smiled. This lady was just as crazy as I was and all about the money.

She stopped fucking my Papa years ago and started fucking with one of his workers just to get them to do what she wants, and he's not the only one she's fucking with. I'm sure my Papa already knew because you can't go this long and not know your wife has been with another nigga for five years. That's crazy as fuck.

It took us a minute to get him down to the basement, but we got it done. Just as we made it back upstairs, my phone was ringing, and it was an unknown caller.

"Hello," I spoke into the phone.

"You ready to see me?" He asked.

"I've been ready. Are you coming to me?" I questioned because I was definitely in need of some dick since Lynx's ass wasn't giving it up. I had so much aggression to get off because this entire thing was stressing me the fuck out. I needed to make sure me and my mom were straight. For years my Papa was just fucking up, so I felt nothing killing him. Me and my mom had already plotted his death so that we could collect on his life insurance, his businesses, and whatever money that's left in his bank account. Now that he's officially named me as the heir to the throne, it's up from here.

"I'll see you soon, baby." I was grinning from ear to ear. He wasn't what I wanted in Lynx, but he would have to do until I could get Lynx to see things my way.

CHAPTER 12
Gabe

It's been a few weeks now and things have been quiet. My nerves were still on ten though because quiet didn't necessarily mean shit was good. In fact, it could be that things were about to go to shits. I was hoping not though. Those Heshems have been haunting my muthafuckin dreams. We were at Julez's crib because Juju was in town, and he wanted all of us to come over. The shit has been hanging over our heads long enough, and I was hoping we could finally get to the bottom of it. The shit has been hanging over our heads long enough, and it's time to get to the bottom of it.

"We definitely need to keep an eye on that bitch! She has threatened to kill Malayah and that alone has me on edge. When it comes to my wife and her safety, I'll pop this bitch in her dome and spend the rest of my life in jail!"

"Wheeewww! That baby loves his wife, wit' his sexy fine

ass!" Grams is the only woman I know that has a husband, and still calling the men in her family fine. Especially the newcomers. If she doesn't stamp them into the fine nigga committee, they can't be in the family.

"Urgggghhhh! I just can't get through this one firewall! Remi and I have been working on getting in this shit for weeks!" Just as he said that Cam, Remi and the kids came walking into the family room and the staff were taking their luggage upstairs.

"Sup, nephew! Rem, you look like you ready to have them babies, girl," Zelan told her.

"I am, Uncle Z." She smiled.

"Oh, my goodness, what are you guys doing here? This is the best! I have all of my grandbabies here. Ohhh, Juelz, we have to take a family picture! I'm going to get our stylist, makeup, photographer here for us to do it on Sunday." Ci was so damn excited, and Ma was shaking her damn head, so I knew some shit was about to come out her mouth.

"Ciera, I would have thought that as you got older, your brain cells would smarten you the hell up. I mean, over time you've had your smart moments but today, just ain't one of them. Your husband and children, all the way down to Bill Gates, your son-in-law and daughter in-law as well are about to go to jail at Rikers on a double life sentence. Yo' ass gon' be out here screaming free my man-"

"'Til it's backwards!" I blurted cutting her off, as I sat and ate my damn honey buns. "Y'all know these meetings always be running over and in between lunch or dinner all the damn time.

Ju, you need to serve us summin' to eat. Yo' ass too damn rich not to share your food!" I fussed.

"The chef is making Italian for lunch. She just texted me and said everything will be ready in thirty minutes," Juju stated, and I was ready to eat.

"That's what I'm talking about." I smiled, stuffing the last of my honey bun in my mouth. Ma appeared with a big brown box and plopped in the middle of the floor, and I was trying to figure out when her ass had even gon' and got that damn box or where the fuck it came from.

"Ok, I decided to make these for y'all and being that I put so much thought into this shit, hopefully they let me send them to you. Ma bent over and began shuffling through the box and all eyes were on her. If she was going to pop up with another damn monkey, I knew something!

"When I realized shit wasn't looking good, I pulled out my old faithful and made y'all some shirts." She said to us alarmingly, and I swear Grams passed the shirts out and we started reading them, I personally wanted to feed her ass to her own muthafuckin' gators in her zoo.

"You crazy as hell! I'm not wearing this shit!" Zelan blurted, and Meek ass was on the floor. This shit was definitely a nostalgic moment 'cause Ma can kiss my ass on this shit right here. She had our pictures on the front of the shirt with a Tiara on our head and our names on the back. Juelz shit said, '*Lil Juicy Booty Ju.*' All the shirts read the same thing, she just changed the names at the end. All except mine. My shit said,

'Sweetbox Gabrielle.' Then I noticed that Kari and Myia shirts were all cute and shit.

"Grams, you neva miss wit' it." Cam dapped her ass up while he was trying to catch his breath.

"Nigga, shut up before I shoot you in them hundred million dollar legs and guess what? Uncle Z never fuckin' miss!"

"That or I'll burn them lil' bitches off to nubs and yo' lil' hehe laughing ass will be hopping 'round the stadium as the damn water boy." I was ready to dropkick his ass right along with his grandma.

"Y'all betta leave me alone, 'cause I had a gift for y'all. But keep on, and I'ma let my lil' man go play his damn X-box with his cousins," Cam said to us, and JuJu crazy ass dropped to his knees.

"Yesss! Oh, yesss!" JuJu yelled out. One thing Cam was against was using his son for any illegal dealings. He didn't want his kids in that light at all, and I understood it because we all wanted that for our kids. It's just sometimes it doesn't work out the way you plan it. You can see the sigh of relief over all of us, because none of us wanted to ask him to do that. Juelz and Ciera have always respected their kids' wishes, and Ju even said he would sit in jail before bringing his grandchildren into anything.

"Cam, you know you don't have to do that. We can wait until we figure it out on our own. He's such a smart little boy. I know he will figure out what he's seeing if he finds something," he stated.

"Dad, Cam, Remi and I will be right there to take over as

soon as he gets in. He won't see a thing; I just know if we can't get through this, Kaleb can." JuJu shrugged, and he was right that lil' dude was something special. JuJu already has plans to leave a portion of his security software company to him. JuJu loves that little boy something serious, and he was grooming him right along with his own kids to take over.

"Let me get Lynx on the phone." JuJu called Lynx on Face-Time, and he popped up on the widescreen in the family room.

"The gangs all hear, I see. What's up, y'all. JuJu, tell me you got something. This chick is getting on my nerves, and daily, I'm ready to slit her damn throat. Did you find anything we can use with those names I sent you?" Lynx asked him.

"They were all clean from this, but it looks as if her dad is broke, and owes a lot of people a great deal of money.

"Damn, that's his right hand! These bitches are scandalous. Sorry for my language, ladies. Alonzo made Natalie the heir to the throne last week." He sighed, rubbing the bridge of his nose. I knew this nigga was getting real irritated by all of this.

"We have an ace in the hole finally. My brother has decided to let my nephew help us. His mom just went to get him. Just hang tight." Ju turned back to his computer.

"Ok, I hope this works. It's been a few weeks that I've been here, and I'm ready to light this her ass up and go home!" Lynx was right, this shit was taking long as hell. Ju did say he kept hitting blocks and coming up empty, which was shocking to all of us.

Myah said the nigga wasn't getting any sleep since this started, and they both have been back and forth from Cali to here and back to Mexico. Remi and Kaleb came into the room, and Kaleb was eating a slice of pizza.

"You need me, Uncle J?" He looked over at his uncle.

"Yooo, how old is this kid? He only looks to be about nine or ten years old." Lynx sat up and got closer to the screen.

"Nigga, you are asking the wrong damn questions. You should be asking his lil' ass what's his routing and account number. 'Cause you gon' be able to rock that ho... Oh, ummm, you gone be able to go to sleep in yo' bed by morning. Just know it's going to be a long night," I advised him, and Zelan and Meek were nodding their heads in agreement.

"Kaleb, I'm having a hard time getting through this block. Can you help Uncle J out, and I'll take you to the mall before the weekend is out?" Ju pulled a chair out for him, and this lil' nigga face lit up.

"Shit, he get us what we need you better know I'm breaking the bank on his lil' ass," Zelan added.

"I got five milli with his name on it." We all snapped our necks in Lynx's direction, and he shrugged.

"Like nigga, he said the mall, and you talking about making this lil' nigga rich? You just like this nigga Juelz. Can't never do nothing regular." I laughed because these niggas were too damn extra.

Kaleb sat down in front of the laptops that his uncle had set up, and his little fingers went to work for a good three minutes, maybe four as we sat and watched him in amazement. He stopped and then Ju and Remi jumped in, and their fingers were on the damn move.

"Let me know what time we're going to the mall, Uncle J." This lil dude grabbed the rest of his pizza and left the damn room.

"What's up? Why did he leave?" Lynx questioned.

"'Cause that's Bill Gates the muthafuckin' third!" Ma told him excitedly. "Wheewww! Cam, I should fuck you up! You shoulda been let that baby come here and help these niggas stay free!

"Fuck! Yesss! I got it! Oh, sorry, Mom." Ju jumped up in excitement as he and Remi celebrated.

"Lynx, do you know a Kasharra Jones?" Ju asked him.

"The name sounds familiar. I think that's one of Natalie's friends, and the only reason I know that is because I heard her laughing on the phone the other night and calling the person on the phone Sharra. Another thing that's strange is Alonzo hasn't been around in about a week. The last time I saw him, he was here at the house. Ever since he's made her the heir, she's been on her high horse. Now she's planning our wedding. I was never doing that shit, so I'm glad we're getting somewhere," he communicated.

"An email account from Gmail LC2 sent the video to Natalie, and she sent it to Kasharra Jones, her mother, and about five other people that's related to her in New York. She offered to pay them for holding the video and said if anything happened to her, to turn the video into the Feds. From what I can see, they haven't forwarded it to anyone else. I've just deleted it off the databases. So, you need to get to the person that videoed this because I'm sure that person has it on their phone," Ju revealed, and we were all excited.

"Lynx, even though Ju has found the videos, he's right. We still have to figure out who has the original recording. I believe you also need to dig deep into your organization because somebody that was with us in New York when Malayah was kidnapped, did all of this. We didn't have much security, we didn't have any of ours, and you only had a handful. To be honest with you, it may be someone close to you, and it may not be your security. Ju, have you investigated his family?" Juelz looked over at JuJu.

"Nahhh, I only have a select few in my family that work for me, and they're my brothers. I know my brother and cousins wouldn't do this. None of them are disloyal to this organization." I could hear the irritation in Lynx's voice.

"Son in-law, if shit starts to look fucked up, you gotta start looking at everybody. It's just the way the game is played. Greed will make a muthafucka change up on you, and just because you got the same blood running through your veins, don't make that nigga loyal. You need to cut the snakes off at the head before shit gets worse." I had to try and talk him into letting Ju investigate his brother and cousins. Trust me, I prayed it wasn't them. I need this shit to be over because my damn daughter is hurting over this nigga. I've even called Zayah and asked her to stall this divorce process because I'm riding with Lynx on this one. I knew this shit was hard on him. He may have reacted too quickly, but when you're in panic mode, that's what you do sometimes. Zayah agreed to help me by stalling out because she also believed Layah was acting off emotions.

"Gabe is right. Trust me, we've all had them, and I know hearing us say that shit doesn't make you feel any better, but in this life of sin, it's either gon' be you or them! And if you anything like us, it's always gon' be them!" Zelan also tried getting through to Lynx.

"I think we all need to get into position and start making our way to Mexico. Ju, let me know when you have intel on the security on the compound. That will determine if I need to bring all my girls from the Diamond Clique. We might only need a few of the girls, me and Myah. Jah is already there with Lynx. He's close by, so Lynx has help," Kari stated.

"We already have the floor plan of the compound and the security guards on the compound. I say we move out tomorrow, because we still need to find the mole in his camp. If we make a move too soon, that might alert him," Ju objected.

"He's right, and I need to handle everybody she sent the video too. I got that part. I appreciate y'all for stepping in and helping get this resolved. I'll let you know when their heads have been sent," Lynx added, and I had to look at this crazy nigga.

"Nigga, that's why we in this shit now!" I shook my damn head. We were all ready to get this shit over with and get back to our lives. Even Meek was ready to take this flight with us.

"Run it, Ju. Let me know what you find. Do me another favor. See if you could run the cameras back a week to see if Alonzo left the compound. One of the guards said he never saw him leave. Oh yeah, Pop tell my wife I love her, and I'll see her soon." He smiled at me.

"Nigga, you call and tell her angry, grumpy ass that shit. Anything regarding your name is like saying lawyers ain't shit and ain't never gon' be shit! I'm sick of it! Gotta walk around my house like I'm visiting. Just 'cause y'all having marital problems, ion think that shit should involve the family. It's like if she doesn't like your ass, we not supposed to like you!" We all burst out laughing, and I think we needed it.

"Lawd, I swear, all this seriousness makes me want to get high every other minute. Y'all know I'm about lift off. Gabe, bring yo' ass on before Trixie wakes up from her nap. You know y'all can't smoke together no mo'. My girl's hormones are high as hell now that she's older, and she be trying to get her some Gabe juice every chance she gets. Harry gon' end up beating your ass again, chile."

"Lynx, we'll see you soon, brother. Let us know if you need some assistance with those problems in New York," Juelz offered to him, and then we ended the call.

"That nigga doesn't give a fuck! He about to put his murder game on fleek, and I'm here for all that shit!" Zelan said as we all headed out to go get us some lunch.

A couple of hours later, I was walking in the house, and Malayah was in the family room watching these sob ass girly movies.

"Layah, where is your mom?" I asked her.

"Her and Bray went to meet Melani at Play Zone." She shrugged.

"So, why didn't you go?"

"Because I didn't feel like going, Dad." She sat up from the couch, and baby girl looked like she was just damn lost.

"Put your shoes on, and come on. We're going to hang out for a little while. You need to get out of this damn house, Layah," I told her. If it's one thing I know, that's sitting around looking ugly in the face wasn't going to help your situation. The damn walls were closing in on my baby. All she did these days was tend to demon seed whenever she could pry him from her mama's arms and talk to them damn clients all day.

"Dad! I'm going out with Kari, Melani, Remi, and Laila later tonight." She laid back down and started watching television again, so I walked over and turned the television off.

"Get up! Let's go, and don't talk back to your daddy!"

She huffed and puffed, but she got up and went to go freshen up and I laughed. This was something I needed to do, because my baby needed her dad right now. Her mom said she has talked to her, but she's being so stubborn. Malayah is my baby; she has so much of me in her, so I can understand her stubbornness. Hell, I didn't think I would have ever forgiven Gia for sneaking and meeting up with Melani's pussy ass dad. Especially, knowing that nigga was the one that shot up my car, and she got shot in the process. I love Lani, and everybody knows that's my baby girl, but Layah has my blood running through her. I give her a hard time because that's just our shit. That's the bonding that makes us who were to each other, and today is no different, but I'm going to be there for her. It took her ass forever, but we were finally on our way to where I wanted to take her.

"Dad, we're going to the mall?" She got excited and sat up in her seat.

"Yeah, shopping always makes me feel better, so that's what we're going to do. Layah, before we go inside this mall, let's talk for a minute. I was in a meeting today with the family, and Lynx was in on that meeting. That man loves you, and I know you want to give him a hard time, but he's doing this for all of us. I truly commend that dude for what he's doing.

Many will say or can say his movement was weak, and he just gave in to her. Nah, that nigga is the true definition of a boss. He's giving that bitch a hard ass time. Nothing about your husband is weak. I think we had a breakthrough, because Cam let Kaleb help Ju. They found the videos; now Lynx has to deal with some other shit, because he definitely got a dirty muthafucka in his camp. You don't have to make any decisions now but talk to that man. Hear him out and look at it from his perspective. Now come on, let's go blow a bag." I smiled, she wiped her tears that had fallen, and we got out of the car. The moment we walked past the food court and all her favorite stores, her attitude went from perky to annoyed.

"Nooooo! Why do we have to go to Macy's, Dad?" Her lil' ungrateful ass started, and I was ready to leave her ass right here.

"Layah, shut yo' ungrateful ass up! I brought you here so we can bond. Now, I'm tired of seeing you in them lil' raggedy ass pajamas you keep wearing at the house. Gon' and get you and that boy some clothes. I know you not getting no child support, so I'm helping yo' ass out!" I fussed.

"Dad, I'm tired! I don't feel like doing a lot of shopping! And you do realize I still have access to all of Lynx's accounts and I make over six figures as an attorney, right? I don't need child support," She whined.

"You're right your ass is tired! Just tired as hell 'cause you don't care 'bout nobody damn feelings! Macy's finally gave me my damn credit card back, and I was trying to celebrate with yo' lil' ugly ass. That's why that fine ass crazy bitch got yo' cartel-ish ass husband over there in Mexico rubbing sunscreen on choco-latey skin." I guess our bonding time is over because the lil' heifer stuck her feet out, and I tripped over the clothing rack going into the store. Then the heathen started picking up all kinds of shit that she didn't even need.

"Hey, Mr. Gabe!" Stacey greeted us as we made our way towards the front.

"Hey, Stacey. Where is Christine?" I asked her.

"She's in her office." She laughed because I guess she saw what Layah ass did. I strutted my ass to the back fast as shit, because I had something up my sleeve.

"Christine, I caught this girl stealing. She's out there stuffing clothes in her big LV tote bag. She's about 5'6 in height, light brown complexion, bougie as hell, with big fluffy curly hair. She might favor me but trust me, she's not related to me. Just lock her ass up! She got some damn nerve coming up in our store stealing shit.

Christine, why my damn chair look all dirty and shit?

What's going on with my damn name tag? Chris, you gotta do better 'bout letting people just come in here and mess up our shit. I told you they be using your office when yo' ass not here, and Stacy 'nem ass ain't no help. Anyway, I need you to call them loss prevention people so they can go hem her lil' thieving ass up and call them folks. She's holding a pile of clothes in her arms to throw y'all off." I sat down in the chair as she pulled the cameras up.

"Gabe, is that Malayah?! Oh my God, I haven't seen her in so long. She has grown into such a beautiful woman. Let me get out there and say hello to her. I'm so proud of her and all that she has accomplished in life. Why are you trying to get that baby in trouble? You always got some mess going. Gia told me that all you and Malayah do is argue." She chuckled.

"Christine, how yo' ass gon' just say her ass ain't stealing when I told you she was damn stealing. Her fish mouth ass is thievin' in this damn sto'! And you gon' just let her walk outta here with y'all shit?! I bet you when she goes out tonight, she gon' have some stolen shit on! Macy's shit!" Her ass doesn't ever listen to me when I come in here. She rushed out of the office and over to Layah.

"Malayahhh! Look at you! It's been such a long time since I've seen you. Your mom and dad brag so much about you. They're so proud of you, and so am I. I see you're hanging out with Dad today. Make sure he buys everything you want," she told her.

"I'm not buying her shit, 'cause she done stole half the shit she had in her arms! Ask her to open her bag up." I licked my tongue out at Layah's ass, because she was gon' get this payback.

"Dad! I'm not stealing! You told me to get what I want, and that's what I'm doing. Urgghhhhhh! I swear I'ma get yo' ass back! I can't believe yo' Boweavel ass trying to get me locked up!! I'm telling Mom as soon we get in the car." She mushed me in the forehead, and I jumped because I felt like that was abuse. Touching me unwanted is always a trigger warning for me.

"Hunny, we don't pay your dad any attention in here. He's our highlight of the day. You're a lawyer; we know you wouldn't steal." When Chris told her that, I almost twirled my neck in a circle like my damn grandson been teaching me, because what!

"What the hell does that mean, she's a lawyer, and you know she won't steal! News flash, CHRISTINE! Lawyers lie the best! They asses are trained to lie, taught by the best of the best to lie, get barred to lie, they know you done killed thousands of people and as long as that money is right, they gon' lie with you and for yo' ass! You done got caught with bricks on top of bricks, and that lawyer gon' be right there lyin' they ass off! My client was home with his children and knowing them lil' niggas is the start of the new baby gang bang generation! Probably got AK's and bricks under they damn toddler bed.

Have you seen her last few cases on television? Now, Christine, you and I both know them niggas did that shit. Her ass just lie so well, she gets them off every time.

Look at her ass! She may look innocent but she a liar and now a thief! I'm tired of this back and forth with us, Christine.

Your loyalty should be with me, and if I'm telling yo' black ass, Layah is in here stealing! You supposed to call them folk on her ass! So, they can lock her ass up and throw away the damn key!"

I walked out the door fast as shit and pissed, 'cause I could never have any fun. I wanted to pay her ass back for tripping me up in front of all of them damn people. My payback gon' be next level for her ass 'cause Gabe never forgets. For the rest of the day, we talked shit. She told her mama what I did, and then me and the lil' huzzy even went to Gucci to charge up Lynx's credit with them. I got me a couple of suits, belts, and some shoes. I kinda like when she's mad at that nigga.

CHAPTER 13
Malayah

I was trying to find some normalcy in my life for me and Bray. All I kept thinking about was my life with my husband, and every time my thoughts went in that direction, I almost always went into a panic attack. I was alive but with my heart being shattered into a trillion pieces, I was merely existing. Not to mention Brayden was asking for his dad all the time. Lynx always calls and checks on us, and he talks to Bray daily, but that's not enough for him. He wants to see his dad. I filed for a divorce, but Zayah is saying the courts are backed up. I'm hoping it goes through soon because I just want this all over.

I've said time and time again that I didn't want to be with a street dude, and this is the reason why. I don't have anything against them. I just can't take the emotional rollercoaster that being with a dude of Lynx's caliber takes you on. That shit brings trouble and a lot of pain. Lynx and I were doing alright in our marriage. My only complaint has always been him spending more time at home with his family. We go from that to a bitch trying to take us all down, and now wanting to kill my ass. My uncles and Dad have so much security around me and Bray, it makes me not want to even go outside. Tonight, was different and so needed. This would give me a chance to have a different atmosphere and fulfill my need to have some alcohol in my system.

I can't wait to go hang out with the family tonight at the club. Getting dressed, putting some makeup on, and just looking nice would for sure put me in a better mood than I've been in. I tried to get Bri to get out of the house and come visit me at my parents for a little while. My mom said that she could, but she didn't want to leave in hopes that Malik would at least talk to her. She is going through a tough time with him, and I feel so bad for them. My damn heart almost stopped beating when I saw his ass standing there. I tried to get Bri's attention, but it was too late. He had already heard what she'd said. I was hoping that she had gotten the courage to talk to him because I knew if he found out a different way, the outcome would be different.

Malik and I have gotten really close over the years, so I knew he would take it hard if he found out how she felt. Since this whole Natalie Alvarez bullshit, I haven't talked with him much. I know they were working overtime to figure out how to end her and get to the bottom of who was behind this. When my dad said that Ju had a break in getting the information he

THE CARTER CARTEL: LYNX CARTER

needed, I called him to see if there was anything that me and my investigative team could do to help. He said he was having trouble coming up with the owner because the IP address was coming up being created in our home. It was being used at Nori's, Malik's, and Aunt Nae's house, and I found that shit strange.

So, my family's theory was right. The person behind all this was someone close to Lynx, and I prayed to God it's not Malik. Because his attitude lately has been on a thousand, and that's with everyone Bri told me. I tried to call him a couple of days ago to check on him, but he's yet to call me back. Just the thought of someone that I had grown to love possibly turning on us was enough to make me light-headed. But Ju said it could also be a way for the person to throw us off, by reverting it back to us and I was praying that was the case. So, I'm not going to blame him for anything. I'm just going to keep my eyes open to all of them. I just wanted this shit over with. My son can't even go out and have a normal life because of this bullshit. If I could, I would kill this Natalie bitch myself! However, tonight, I was putting all of my marital and family drama to the back of my brain.

"Babe, what time are you girls leaving tonight?" My mom walked into my room with Brayden running behind her.

"Kari said they would be here at ten to pick me and Lani up. Lani and the kids are staying the night here since Mano is out of town." My dad is going to blow a gasket when he realizes all of his grandkids will be here, and him and mom have to babysit.

"Lawd, that means I have to get an attitude with your dad over my grandkids. Every time they're here, he picks with them damn babies." My mom sighed, and I laughed.

"No one takes my dad seriously when it comes to our kids. We know that he's joking, and for some odd reason, every last one of them loves his old ass to death. And as much shit as he talks, we know he loves them and us."

My birthday is in a couple of days, and I don't have any plans for it. Before all of this shit happened with Lynx, I had an entire list of shit I wanted to do. I asked him if he would take me to Bali, and he said he would take me wherever I wanted to go. I'm not going to even sit here and lie; I miss the fuck out of my husband. But I refuse to just allow him to treat me any kinda way. Having him just come in and make final decisions without even consulting me is just disrespectful. If the tables were turned, that nigga would've gone on a killing spree.

If he's over there doing him, no matter the situation, I'ma be over here doing me. I've thought about him being with her sexually, and that shit drives me crazy. The way that man handles me in the bedroom, of course imagining him with another woman, would have me like this. That shit pisses me the fuck off. Just the image of him sucking on her pussy had me fuming. Being put deep in my feelings, I picked up, I sent his ass a text.

Me: I hate your ass!

Husbae: And I love everything about you. You're my air!

Me: Nigga, this is not the time for all your fake ass real nigga quotes! I should have been your air the day you chose to go with that bitch! Now, bye! I'm going out to find my future!

Husbae: That's yo word?

Me: Is pussy pink?

Husbae: Say less.

I blew out an exaggerated sigh and got off the bed so that I could start getting ready for the night. I did find me a nice lil' bodycon dress out of Macy's that I just love, so I'm going to match it up with a strappy sandal by Christian Louboutin. I still had to do my makeup and hair. Darius was coming over tomorrow to do my mom's hair, and I was definitely jumping in his chair after her. I've been sitting around in a sucky mood, and tonight all that stops. I'm going to enjoy myself and my family. Next week I plan to go back to Puerto Rico and pack the rest of my things.

I haven't decided on my living arrangements or where I want to be, because I have a really good setup in Puerto Rico. Aunt Nae called me earlier asking for Bray, so I'm going to drop him off over there with her tomorrow. With my head consumed with all this bullshit plus my workload increasing by the days, I was glad my son had people that loved on him while his mommy wasn't herself. It truly does take a village.

A couple of hours later, I was adding some finishing

touches to my hair, and I heard a knock at the door, and it was Lani coming in looking good as ever.

"Okkkkkk! Look at my good sis! I see you, boo! We gon' show our ass a little bit tonight! I already told Mano I'ma be a rachet housewife tonight!" she laughed, gyrating her body.

"I might find somebody's son to let off some of this aggression." I shrugged and that stopped Lani from her antics.

"Girl, your ass is married, and that man is coming back to you. Why are you acting this way? Listen, baby sis. I get it, and to a certain extent, I understand it. You knew who he was when you jumped in and stayed in your marriage. You decided to take the good, bad, and the ugly, and right now, you're dealing with the ugly. He explained himself; he just didn't do it on your time. I think you should at least have a conversation with him when this is all over. I'm not going to say that I wouldn't be mad, but I would definitely get over it and pray that my man walks out of this shit alive."

"I don't give a fuck! That nigga fucked up, not me! He made me single, and I'm damn sure going to see what my single ass can get into!" I grabbed my purse and walked out the room with her behind me. By the time we made it downstairs, Kari, Laila, Remi, and Myah were in the kitchen eating some pound cake my dad made.

"Uncle Gabe, this cake is slamming! I swear you need to open a bakery," Laila greedy ass mumbled as she stuffed more cake into her mouth.

"Where y'all going?" My dad questioned.

"We're headed to the club; it's time to twerk a little." Kari started twerking while Lani was hitting her on the ass, and my dad was standing there with the stank face.

"Y'all too old to be plopping that evaporated booty y'all think y'all got around. And why every time we go to the club, y'all gotta go to the damn club. Well, Layah mad at her baby daddy 'cause he over there with the Blaxican Meg Thee Stallion, so y'all blow a bag on his ass tonight and don't come asking me for shit. I need all my money for Sunday morning service. Gotta pay my hundred dollars to my dues." He shook his head.

"I thought you're supposed to give ten percent of your earnings and to my knowledge, your earnings are millions. SO, you out here cheating the house of the lawd?" I asked him.

"Mind yo' damn business! I ain't cheating no damn body! The lawd know my heart. If I give all to Mount Calvary's pastor and his wife, then what me and Gia gonna have? Hell, y'all always running your tired grown asses home with all these fucking bay bay kids so I need my money to be able to keep paying taxes on this here property and keep the damn fridge stocked. I ain't got no money for paster to take and go shine his gold ceilings. You know sister Shirley said everything gold in paster house. Yeah, he won't get mine. They betta take this hundred and put a praise on it!" When he threw his hands in the air, we all fell out laughing. This man was plum fool.

"Dad, why you not staying home to help Mom with the kids?" Lani asked, getting up from her seat.

"Hell to the nawl! Your kids are bad as hell; they get that shit from Mano side. I saw the girl throwing up gang signs, and the boy came and asked me for some baking soda. You betta watch they ass! They probably setting up shop in the pool house for the rest of the drug dealer's kids. And I'm not gon' even get started on her child! That lil' nigga is possessed! I thought we was gon' have to go to jail, so I asked him to teach me how to stare straight ahead without breaking the stare and twirl my head around in a circle. It's just hard to watch him do that shit and not want to run. I gotta go, Uncle Truth is outside."

"I can't stand his ass," I blurted 'cause he had us all in here on the damn floor.

"Uncle Gabe remains undefeated and top muthafuckin' tier! He gon' always come for us and our damn kids." Laila laughed.

"If he didn't, I would be worried and think he was sick." Lani laughed, and we all headed out to the awaiting trucks. Now that Kari and Laila were with us, our security detail was extra thick. The family didn't want to take any chances with all that was going on. Traffic was a little heavy, so it took about forty-five minutes to get to the club.

"Damn, it's crazy packed in here tonight," Laila said as we all moved through the club to VIP. *Put It On Da Floor* by Latto feat. Cardi B was blaring through the speakers. We made our way to our section, and immediately got our drinks ordered. There was a big party going on that had all of the sections blocked off with the exception of the Kassom sections.

Twerkulator By City Girls came blasting through the speakers, and our asses was going the fuck in. I mean, we showed our damn ass, garnering the attention of the dudes next to us. One dude stood off to the side, and his eyes were on me, so I gave him a show. The DJ was going in, and we were drinking and going the fuck off, just having a good time. Our dads were in the club shaking their heads, but they let us have our fun. We we're a hot commodity tonight, there were about four guys that walked over to us. Kari tried to send them away, and I invited Mr. Sexy with the suckable lips to have a drink with me. As soon as *Twerk* by City Girls Feat. Cardi B came on, I was on my feet killing it, and he was right behind me, dancing on my ass. When I turned in the direction of my dad, with a scold on his face, his ass did what he does best; record what the hell was going on. Really dad? I mouthed and stopped twerking. I still had my back pressed to ole boy's front.

"Nah, don't stop now!"

My dad came close and held his camera with his right hand and pointed at me with his left.

"This shit is going global. You want to be a city girl so bad? I'm DMing this shit to Diddy. He likes em round your age and skin tone anyway. You kinda look like that damn Careesha girl. This right here is yo potential tape! You might not need a cartel boss after all. Love Combs is a billionaire! Ain't that's his new name, everything is love or some shit! Well, we gon' love his damn money, I'll never have to worry about paying my hundred-dollar Tithe again! All you got to do is get used to golden showers, cause that's what I heard he likes." Ignoring my dad, I continued dancing. I didn't give a damn; my husband wanted to pretend he wasn't married, so, so was I. My dad went back to where he was standing but he was still recording. If I had something to throw at his ass, I swear I would slang that shit right at his throat wit his peanut ass head.

"Damn, you fine as fuck, shorty. What's your name?" He asked, pulling me into him.

"Malayah, what's yours?" I asked him.

"Rock. You got a man, Malayah?" He inquired.

"I mean, legally I do, but he doesn't think so, so it's whatever," I explained as we stood near the railing watching the people party on the first level.

"I don't give a fuck about that nigga, just wanted to see where your head was at. The next nigga doesn't concern me, baby girl. Come on over and chill in my section with me before you get up out of here. It's my birthday, and this is my birthday party." He smiled.

"Happy birthday! I have a birthday coming up too, but I'll make sure I stop by your section before the night is over." We spoke for a few more minutes, I hugged him, and he headed back to his section.

"Girl, you trying to get hemmed up."

"You better stop playing with Lynx," Laila said to me as I poured another drink.

"I'm trying to tell you; you know these men we're married to is crazy as hell." Lani shook her head as the waitress sat a blue Hawaiian, and some wings in front of her.

"Ewwww, I want one of those," I said to her as I picked up one of her wings.

"Bring her ass some wings, 'cause you not 'bout to sit here and eat up my shit," Lani fussed, and we all fell out laughing.

I saw Mr. Suckable head out of VIP, and he blew me a kiss. Damn, that lil' nigga was fine as fuck. He wasn't my husband by far, but his hazel eyes complimented his caramel complexion, and I'm not gone talk about his cut-up ass body, muscles, and tatts everywhere.

"Wheeewww! He fine as hell, but he not worth the trouble." Laila sipped on her drink, shaking her head at the situation. For the next couple of hours, we kept the drinks flowing, ate, and partied. I stood up to look over at the first floor, and it was packed, but I could have sworn I saw Lynx and Nori moving through the crowd. I continued looking in the direction I thought I saw them in, but I didn't see them. Brushing it off, I sat back down and enjoyed time with my family. After about forty five minutes, I looked over at Rock's party, but never saw him come back and still didn't see him in his section. Some of his friends were huddled up talking. Some of them had concerned looks on their faces, and some left out of the section in a hurry. My phone lit up, and I saw that it was Lynx texting me.

Husbae: One thing I don't pay about
is respect! I try my best to give that
to you, but the shit I'm dealing with
is a little bit different. I haven't so
much as touched this bitch, yet you
sit in a public club and disrespect
me?! When I tell you not to fuck with
me, that's what the fuck I mean! And
when I say every nigga that
breathes the same air, every nigga
that touches you in any sexual way
will die, that's what the fuck I mean!

The next text had me screaming and throwing my damn
phone down to the floor. It was a picture of Rock with his head
severed, sitting right next to his body on a conveyer belt.

"What's wrong?" Kari questioned as they all jumped up.
My dad and uncles ran over, and I was a complete mess. Kari
grabbed my phone off of the floor, passed it to my dad, and he
showed it to my uncles. They ushered us out of the VIP section
with our guards following behind us.

"It's time for y'all to get home. Malayah, he's just a little
upset. You were acting up a little and dealing with someone as
powerful as Lynx, you have to move a little different," Uncle
Juelz tried to get me to understand.

"Ion know where yo' ass get that the nigga is a little upset
from! 'Cause that nigga head is no longer apart of his body, and
he got one eye going to north of his east and the other one is
looking straight head. Damn! Y'all think he was keeping his eyes
on both his killers?"

"Yooo, excuse me, shawty. You were talking to my cousin

inside. Have you seen him?" The guy I saw with Rock earlier asked me. Putting my poker face on, the face that led me to many wins in the courtroom.

"No, I haven't. The last time I saw him was inside a couple of hours ago." I shrugged.

"You sure? You look upset about something. You good?" he asked, taking a step closer, but my dad moved in front of me.

"Be lucky you got that and move on." My joking dad had disappeared, and the real Gabe showed up.

"Nigga, I'll move when the fuck I'm done asking this bitch about my cousin!" That was the end of the conversation when dude pushed my dad. The punches my dad was throwing was eating dude up. One of his boys tried to jump in it, and security gripped him up. Dad was beating his ass so bad blood was everywhere. Dude wasn't even fighting back anymore.

"Pussy ass nigga, call my daughter a bitch again!" My dad yelled as they pulled him away.

"Y'all go home!" Uncle Juelz said as he walked off to go check on my dad. I couldn't believe this shit was happening. I can't believe Lynx did this shit and killed that boy for nothing! Oh my God, what the fuck have I done!

CHAPTER 14

Lynx

This girl takes me for a joke, and I hate I had to show her this side of me. I've never raised my voice at my wife before, so I know she's an emotional wreck. I've never given her this side of me. Maybe that's something her ass needed to see. You can only tell a person who you are, and they will either believe you or not. But if you show them, then their outlook on you might be different, and the outlook I wanted her to have tonight is not to ever fuck with me! When she texted me that I hate you shit, I had just landed in the city because I had to handle these muthafuckas that had possession of these videos.

Since having that talk with Juelz and his crew, I wanted to make sure I handled this shit myself. Malik is in Puerto Rico dealing with his personal shit with Bri, so I decided to have Nori ride this out with me and just Nori. No Mel, no security, just

Nori. When she sent that bullshit ass text, I knew when she said they were going out that she was going to Juelz & Zelan's club. So, I called Gabe, and after I promised to pay him ten racks for his information, he confirmed it. I gave my father in-law the money because I wanted to. I could've found that information from my security team that's guarding her. She thinks they belong to Juelz, but that's all me.

I was in the club and watched her show her ass. Once that nigga touched her, my eyes were on him. As soon as he left the VIP area, Nori spotted him, and we followed him out to the parking lot. Good thing for us, he was walking to his car, so we gripped his bitch ass up and took him to out warehouse. I'm not to be fucked with, and I mean that shit!

Nori looked over at me as we moved through the city. "You know you gotta go check on her, right??"

He knew that I was mad as hell right now, so checking on her twerking ass wasn't in my plans.

> Wifey: How could you do that?! It was his birthday! You're such a heartless bastard! He was innocent and did nothing wrong! We were just dancing. I can't stand you!

I chuckled 'cause baby girl was pissed. She knew what she was doing. I warned her, and she neglected to listen to what I had it say. So, it is what it is.

> Me: You played in my face, and that's that.

I thought about her text and dialed her up on FaceTime. I knew my emotional ass wife, and she better not be over there crying over that nigga.

"What do you want?" She screamed, and just as I thought, her eyes were puffy and red.

"So, you're over there crying over a dead nigga!" Her orange manicured nails covered her mouth as if she was trying to prevent her scream from being heard. I hated to see my wife in such a state, but she had to know that consequences came with reckless behavior.

"Leave me the fuck alone!" She angrily spat and hung up the phone.

"Your ass is crazy as fuck! But I feel you on that shit. Ain't no nigga gon' ever be able to speak after digging in my bitch! And if she's my wife or I consider you that, it's a wrap!" Nori adjusted in his seat. He's just been in a shitty mood ever since that Tasha shit.

"Have you figured out how you wanna handle the Tasha situation?" I asked him.

"Nah, net yet. I've been with this woman for fifteen years, and I'm still trying to wrap my head around that bullshit. Tasha been down with what I have going on for a long ass time, and even though I'ma busy nigga, I make sure I handle home. I never leave my girl to wonder about shit. The crazy part is I was about to propose to her. I had Tianna set everything up, and then this shit happened a few days before. You were right about her developing feelings for the nigga; I was just too embarrassed to admit it. She screamed and cried over his dead body, and it took everything in me not to kill her.

Bruh, to hear her crying out for another nigga, hurt me to my core. I can't do the relationship shit no more, man. That getting in a relationship shit is dead. I'll dig in some guts, but that's all shorty gon' get from me. With the type of life a nigga live, I can't be worried about what my woman is doing, when I'm not home. Shit so crazy how you can give a bitch the world and she still go fuck with a nigga that can't even buy her a fucking plastic globe. I can't be worried about what my woman is doing when I'm not home.

Anyway, I think Tasha good on talking. I threatened her family, and she loves the shit out of them, so I knew she wasn't going to talk. You're right though; a dirt nap is needed. I'll do it on my time." He sighed, looking out of the passenger window as we moved in and out of the city streets. I wasn't going to question him on the shit further because I knew his heart was heavy and that Tasha was a sore spot. He was right though, when he was ready, he would do what the fuck needed to be done. Shit was gone be hard as a muthafucka though.

It felt good to be driving. I didn't do it often but loved it when I did. Always having security around you and them driving me around can get overwhelming sometimes. So, I love the times when I can just relax and do me. Something as simple as pushing my own wheels always brought me back to the beginning. The days when I was so fucking hungry for this shit that I was selling crack rocks out my sock. Now, a nigga had a whole fucking empire.

Kasharra Jones was the last person on our list, and I pulled down the block from her crib. I wanted to get to them as quick as I could, because once Natalie and her little fuckin' puppets realize the videos have been deleted, she may still use the original video. We slipped on our gloves and masks as we moved up to her front door. It took Nori a few minutes, but he unlocked the door and killed the alarm. His ass is loving the new devices Juju gave him. We went inside, and it sounded as if she was on the phone upstairs.

"Nat, you gotta make sure this shit is airtight, baby. How long do I have to be here? I'm ready to be there with y'all. Does he know that you killed your dad?" She asked, and there was a pause. Nori and I decided to sit and listen to the conversation. Maybe we could get some information.

"No, he doesn't know that, Sharra. He thinks he's on a business trip, and that's the way I'm going to keep it. To be honest, I only want him to sign his organization over, and that happens on Monday. Once he signs his name on the dotted line, that video will be sent to the Feds, and we'll have all of them out the way. Santiago Vega is old; we will take over this shit, and I can't fuckin' wait!" It was a plus that this bitch had Nat on speaker. Hearing Natalie say that lets me know that this bitch gotta die ASAP! She was going to turn it over to the cops anyway. That's some wild shit.

"Is he still asking for a drug test on Siani?" Sharra questioned.

"Yeah, but it'll be too late to even care." She sighed.

THE CARTER CARTEL: LYNX CARTER

"Let her end the call. If she lets off that something is wrong, that will alert Natalie," Nori whispered.

"My flight leaves early; I'll see you tomorrow." Kasharra ended the call with her. Now that I was in Kasharra's presence, it looks like she could fill me in on some shit I've been wondering about. Nori eased the door open, and she immediately jumped up. When she made a move for her gun, Nori ended her. The silencer split her head open, splattering brains on the back of her headboard. Her slump body hit the floor. She was in this bitch in a bra and panties. Dead as hell now.

"Fuckkkkk! I wanted to ask her some shit, nigga!" I was mad as fuck right now.

"My bad, she went for her shit. We've been in and out on all the others; I thought it was the same, nigga." H shrugged, looking around the room for laptop, and cell phone. He ran a device on both of them, so that it wouldn't trace back to any of our locations. JuJu wanted us to bring them to him.

"Yo, hold up!" I said to him as we were walking out. A picture on the wall in the bedroom next to hers caught my attention. It was a big portrait of Natalie's daughter, and Kasharra. On the other walls, there were pictures of Kasharra in the hospital holding her newborn.

"This is Natalie's kid, but from these pictures, it looks as if Kasharra gave birth to her." I looked over at Nori, confused as fuck.

"So, do you think this is her kid?" I couldn't answer him because I had no clue.

"I don't know, but this shit is weird as fuck. I mean she calls

Natalie mommy, and look at her, she looks like me, and I know I haven't fucked Kasharra. Never seen her before."

"Maybe she's the god mom or something. Now why her ass up in the bed like that baby is hers, I don't know. Maybe she has her own baby, and that kid is hers. Look, let's get out of here and figure this out tomorrow." When we walked out the door, Nori saw the cleanup crew parked up the street and went up to talk to them for a minute. Once I dropped Nori off at home, I decided to head over to see my wife. This shit with Nat was getting weirder and weirder. I just hoped after her ass is dead, no more bitches that done sat on my dick comes out the wood works. I'm getting too old for all this Bad Boys shit.

When I got there, I did a retina scan, and the gates opened. I saw security walking the grounds, and I'm glad they're on their jobs. I dialed Gabe's number because I didn't just want to walk into the house this time of the morning. That nigga'll probably start shooting and ask who the fuck is it afterwards.

"Hello." His groggy voice came through the phone.

"Yo, Pop. Come open the door for me."

"Mmmm, mmmm, come back tomorrow." I had to pull the phone away from my damn ear.

"Nigga, tomorrow?! I flew all the way here from Mexico to see my wife. Come open the door, man." I knew this nigga was about to give me a hard time.

"No, nigga! You came over here to be a serial killer! Done scared my poor baby the hell up, and this shit right here gon' cost you! Got me out here fighting to protect my daughter 'cause she married a nigga that can't fight!" He fussed, but I could hear him moving around. A few minutes later, he opened the door.

"Nigga, my fight game is on point. You don't even believe that shit." When I laughed, I knew he was about to show his ass. Bray was walking down the stairs, in his spider man pajamas, his pants being a little crooked and the minute Gabe turned, he walked past him without acknowledging either of us. Gabe ass was standing here with his damn mouth agape, and I knew he was about to let it rip. I swear we gotta get this sleep-walking shit under control with Bray.

"All hell to the fuck nawl! That lil' nigga got the spirits moving all through his ass! I'ma 'bout to wash his ass in this jug of holy oil, and if his ass get to sizzling, y'all gotta go. I'm sicka going to sleep with one damn eye open every night! This shit is stressful! The other damn night I was on the damn couch sleep, so I popped my eyes open 'cause I could just feel when a nigga looking at me. And this lil' pisspot, bugaboo ass nigga was staring at me like his possessed ass was trying to snatch my damn soul!" This nigga had me crying laughing! My baby got his ass shook!

"I done told yo' ass to stop talking 'bout my son. That's your grandson. One of these days, he's going to pay your ass back for always fuckin' with him and his mama," I told him.

"Dad, what's going on?" Melani asked, coming down the stairs, and Malayah was right behind her.

"Urggghhhh! Leave!" She turned around and rushed back upstairs.

"Sup, Lani." I kissed her cheek and went upstairs with Bray

135

in my arms. I had to get him relaxed and put him back to sleep before I went to deal with Malayah. It took me an hour to get him back to sleep, and when I went into Layah's bedroom, she was already asleep. I wasn't able to stay long. I have somebody on the compound that I was able to get to help me out and keep me updated on Natalie's movements. He's the one that she orders to follow me and shit. I'm so damn glad that he was easily swayed. All it took was some paper for the nigga to fold like an origami. She treats her workers like shit, and the money I gave up brought him over to my side. Now when this shit is said and done, he gotta die because if you can't be loyal to her, you damn sure can't be loyal to me. I could hear my wife lightly snoring, and that was the best fuckin' sound I've heard in weeks.

"I'm just here to hold you, lil mama, that's all. I miss the fuck out of you, and I can't wait to make this all up to you." I kissed her lips and then her forehead. I chuckled because tonight must have really worn her out. She really had fallen asleep on me, so I decided not to wake her up. I got undressed and just held her for a little while. And before I knew it, I had drifted off to sleep. The sun was peeping through, which caused me to jump up.

"Fuck!" I had to get going. Easing out of bed and putting my clothes on, I tried to move without waking Malayah up. Once I got myself together, I kissed her lips and headed out the door. I walked into Bray's room, but he wasn't in the bed, and I got concerned. Gia came walking up the stairs.

"Hey, he's in our room asleep. Lynx, how are you holding up? Are you alright out there?" She asked.

"I'm holding on, trying to clear this up and get back to my family. Thank you for taking care of them for me. Ma, I love your daughter and this family." I sighed.

"I know you do, and we love you too. Be safe, and if you need me to come tag that bitch up, I got you." She laughed, and I had to laugh too because I heard my mother in-law still had them hands.

CHAPTER 15
Malik

Three Days Later

We got to Mexico a few hours ago and were waiting on Lynx to give us the green light. We took care of everything that needed to be done. Everybody that had a copy of that video is dead, and it was time to end this bitch, Natalie. Shit took longer than it should but as long as this bitch is handled that time didn't go in vain. Lynx said her compound is heavily guarded, so we needed to get in undetected because he didn't want her alarm. He did pull a couple of her people on our side, and they were helping him on the inside.

She didn't want any of Lynx's security to come with him, so he didn't have them to help him. We damn sure got an army on this side of the gate. These damn Diamond Clique chicks don't play. They ready to put they murder game down. I had to get my mind right and put me and Bria shit to the side. It was time we handled this situation and get back to our lives. This bitch had the team on edge for weeks, and that's unlike us. We usually are able to catch shit before it happens or the moment it does, but this bitch slithered right up under our noses. However, even the slimiest of snakes can be beheaded. We were now on our way to the house that Juelz was renting for us to set up in.

"How long before we move on them niggas?" Mel asked.

"Don't know yet. Lynx gon' make that call and let us know."

Lynx said he would call when it's time. All I know is before we leave Mexico, every muthafucka that had anything to do with this shit or has a problem with The Carter Cartel is going to regret the day they fucked with us.

"Lynx is calling!" Ju yelled out and everyone moved into the room he was set up in.

"Hey, we're all here," Ju told him.

"Good, she's acting a little weird. I think it's because she can't get into touch with her friend. Look, let's get this shit over with; I'm good on this side. Can't wait to see y'all on the other side of the wall. I feel like a nigga 'bout to get out of jail." He ended the call, and we were hype as hell. I ain't never been this fuckin' excited to kill a bitch.

"Let's go do some muthafuckin' damage!" Zelan stated, and I was ready. All that shit talking, and investigating was over. This bitch came to us all big and bad, and we let her ass, now it's our muthafuckin' time. Playtime is over, and I don't think she's ready for what's about to come her way. The Kassom family is a fuckin' wrecking bomb. The way these niggas are strapped up, the shit was crazy as fuck to watch. For as long as I've known them, we never had to get down like this. My phone was ringing. This damn sure wasn't the time to take any calls, but when I saw that it was Lynx, I quickly answered.

"Sup, you good?" I asked him.

"Bro, I just wanted to make sure you're good. I know you got a lot on your mind, but coming into this bullshit, I need you to have a clear mind. If you are not good, bro, sit this one out. I'm gon' be alright, regardless. We're both going through some shit right now, but I need you to be a hundred when you come through them gates."

I had to pull the phone from my ear and look at it. My brother knew me better than anyone, so him saying this shit was pointless. No matter what the fuck I'm going through, I can always put personal aside for business.

"I promise I'm good. Ma would come down from heaven and kill me if I let you do this without me being there to protect you." I laughed.

"Yo' ass is right; she would kick your ass. However, I just didn't want to be insensitive. This my mess to fix up, I'm just grateful that you've been by my side through it all. I won't feel no type of way if you had to watch from the side lines."

I appreciated my brother in more ways than one, but again, him worrying about my mental was wasting time that we didn't have.

"Nigga, your problems are my problems. On mommy, I'm good."

Lynx went silent for a minute before sighing.

"Appreciate you, G. See you in a min. Family first."

"'Til the casket drop." I ended the call.

I thought about what he said, and for a minute, I just took some time to ease my mind. I wasn't concerned about my personal life right now, but I still just needed to relax just for a moment. When people said the streets didn't sleep, I didn't realize how true it was until I was deep in them. It seemed like there was always something. Always a person plotting. Always an enemy lurking. Always a situation that needed handling. I was born for this shit but it could be draining as fuck sometimes. It was a never-ending cycle. After a moment of silence, I said a quick prayer, and then I was ready to go.

We loaded up in our vehicles, and Gabe ass came running out with his fire gun. I know we be having some illegal ass forearms but ever since Lynx married into this damn family, I be having to question how the hell they be able to get their hands on some of this shit. Like, a whole damn fire gun? Then, this nigga was wearing a black polo hoodie and matching joggers that he made sure to let us know he got from the new arrivals section in Macy's. He better have hoped his new fit was fireproof and if it wasn't I hoped he knew how to stop drop and roll. *This nigga is gon' burn these people shit down.* I guess it's not going to matter because they asses about to die.

It took us about twenty minutes to get to the area of the Alavarez compound, and from the scope Ju has on the property, that shit was huge. We all got out of the cars to talk over our plan.

"Lynx has a guard at the front gate who's going to let us on the property. After that, it's more than likely going to be some gunplay. Me, Jah, and the Clique will lead y'all in, then we will disappear and see y'all inside," Kari spoke, and I was very impressed because I had heard a lot about these ladies. They were all fine as hell but to know they were some stone cold killers behind those girl next door looks they possessed was mind boggling. I guess I'm about to see them in action. I saw a little bit of what Kari and Myah could do in New York; they don't play about their family.

"You guys stay focused when we go inside. Lynx is going to do his best to create a path for us. Let's move out." Juelz pulled his guns from his waist, and we moved to the compound. Myah stopped us right before we got to the gate and started passing out goggles. She said that it would help us see in the dark, and all I could think about was these girls needed to be on our squad full damn time. I didn't even think about no shit like that. A nigga like me would have went in that bitch squinting my eyes, knocking shit over and some more. Once we were all in position, Kari and her girls moved in, and the gate opened right up for us with no issues. Even JuJu had his backpack on his back and his AK in his hand. This nigga gave you the best of both worlds. The property was nothing short of astonishing, but I expected nothing less. This bitch was living like royalty. Seven figure cars lined the fucking driveway and I wanted to key some of them bitches just for the hell of it. We made it in without a hitch but, just as we thought the coast was clear, a shot went off. One of the girls had fired at someone and the damn blood splashed on Gabe. He almost dropped his damn fire gun from trying to dodge his new set from getting dirty.

"See, this is why I don't like killing people with they ass. Every time we together, I always be the one getting hit with the blood. On my new fucking set at that! God don't like ugly, and he ain't too fond of ungodly gun totin' ass killas! You owe me a gift card! I need my shit replaced," he fussed, but she ignored his ass as we rushed through the grounds. Before we could make it to the door, the girls from the Diamond Clique had cleared the way. There was a big bulky hispanic guy standing at the door waving us in his direction. Once we all got inside, he led us to the part of the house we needed to be in, and Lynx was waiting for us at the top of the stairs.

"She's on the east wing of the house, and her daughter is on that same side, so we have to be careful. I have someone that's going to get the daughter and care for her."

I drew my head back but bit my tongue. I didn't want to call my brother out in front of all these folk, but the child was his so he should definitely take her in since we were killing her mother. Again, I would never try to lil' boy my brother while we had an audience and even though I hated this Natalie bitch with everything in me, putting his child off on other mutha-fuckas didn't sit right with me.

Lynx knew me like a book so he shook his head and spoke while looking directly at me.

"This entire situation was too damn wild for me to go on

this bitch's word so I was able to pay the nanny to do a swab. I was able to have a rushed DNA test on the little girl, and she's not my child. But I'm confused as to why this kid looks so much like me," he revealed and I was relieved that the girl wasn't his. I did however feel the same way. Why the hell she looks like his ass if it isn't his? Because, she was his fucking twin.

We were led down the hall, and some dude stepped out passing Lynx his guns. "This nigga done came on these people shit and recruited his own team from they damn team! Now that's some hard shit. He's my son in-law when he does smart shit, but when his ass gets to doing all that extra shit, ion know him." Gabe shook his head.

"You think for one second that I was just gon' let you plan to kill me under my roof, nigga? I'm in control of everything that goes on here! I knew you were coming before you got here and look at what we have here. Juelz old ass Kassom, I'm going to have a good time watching you die," Natalie spat, stepping from around the corner. One thing I could contest is that this bitch was bad. Her heels cackled on the marble floors and her ass was dressed in an all-white tailored pants suit with her hair pulled back in a tight bun, showing her exotic features. We'd been killing so many bad bitches lately, the earth was gone be filled with normal hoes in a minute.

"Too bad you'll never get a chance to make that shit happen. One thing I don't do is play with bitches that's not on my playing field. Do you think for one minute that you moved me, just because you had this little information?"

"What yo' ass mean, nigga? I still got it, and if something

happens to me, my people know what to do." She smiled, and Juelz stepped a little closer.

"Nah, see the reason your dumb ass can't get in touch with them is because my nephew here took care of them, and my son here removed all of the videos, including the one from your computer and phone. I play chess, not checkers, baby girl. When you step in the ring with a family like mine, you gotta think outside of the box and ask yourself, what would Juelz Kassom do in a situation like this?

I've gon' a long time in this game trying to do right by my family and the people in our lives. A bitch like you could never takes us down." He nodded his head, and before you could blink good, Kari, her crew, and Jah had taken down every last guard she had standing with her. Blood was every fucking where.

"And then there is Cruella! Girl, where all your people at now? It ain't no damn fun when these niggas got the gun. Mmmmmm, Mmmmm, Mmmmm, let me just feel you in them lil' tall, ungodly looking chicks. They can kill you with the snap of a finger. The head of the crew is Juelz's daughter. Don't step back because you might not ever take another step. And these other niggas... well, you know you tried to go up against them and lost, lawd!" Gabe was on it tonight, and her ass look scared as fuck because one of Lynx's lil helpers brought him a damn chair and I know this shit was about to be a show.

"Nigga, what yo' ass doing? You 'bout to watch television with the bitch or something? Ain't nobody got time for that shit. We kill niggas and get the hell on, 'cause what if they got other family that's coming over to visit and see you in here killing they family? You know how the Mexican and Spanish people do; they be having thirty people in one damn car. Just hurry up and kill this hoe so I can go catch that lil' restaurant down the street from the house. I need me some damn fajitas." Gabe mentioning fajitas made my damn stomach growl. I didn't even notice the damn restaurant but I wasn't above going when we left here.

"I knew it was going to come to this. Come on, Nat. Tell me who put you up to this shit? Look at you; they left you out here to defend yourself. You got all those people killed because you're a money hungry hoe. Y'all killed your pop just because you wanted his policy. It's a lot of shit that comes with greed. I want you to meet somebody."

Lynx waved Kari over and the sinister smile on her face as she took her place next to Lynx even have my ass spooked and I didn't scare easily. This is my cousin Kari. Kari has this lil' juice that I'm so fascinated with. It paralyzes you, but allows you to feel every inch of pain that I'm going to inflict on you," Lynx informed her.

"Fuck you, Lynx! You think this is it! You think the shit stops with me! They're going to kill all of you!" She screamed. Spit spewing from her matted red lips as she tried to lunge at my brother. Before she could yell her next pointless ass threat, Nori took his knife, slid it inside of her, and snatched it out. Then, Kari stuck her needle in Natalie's neck, and that shit must work quick because her ass couldn't move. She almost looked like she was having a silent damn stroke the way her neck was just leaning to the left while she blinked her long ass lashes repeatedly. Nat was just staring and crying. Lynx took his knife and ran it all over her face, and that shit was crazy as she screamed out in agony.

"That's a nice white suit. If the torture squad hadn't got all your blood on it, it would have been a good fit to go meet the Lawd in. You know, I did see one in Macy's that I probably could get during friends and family, I think it's coming up so you might be in luck." Gabe snapped his fingers.

"Awwww damn, I forgot I'm setting this bitch on fire. You won't need a homegoing outfit."

Gabe was a hot mess, but I was eager to see him use that damn gun.

We all stood around watching Natalie scream and cry for the next few minutes and I had to admit, the bitch was a tough cookie. Most folk would have passed out a long time ago. Lynx allowed her to feel that excruciating pain for about thirty minutes, and then he stood from his seat, pulling his gun out and emptying his clip in her ass.

"Let's get out of here," he suggested. A ringing phone had everyone started checking theirs, but it looked as if it was coming from Natalie's body. Lynx bent down, pulled it out of her pocket, and his face instantly scrunched up.

"You good?" me and Nori both asked at the same time. He passed the phone to Nori, and I leaned it to look at what he was talking about.

"What the fuck is that about?" I looked at him in confusion.

"Let's get out of here." He started heading for the stairs.

"Lynx, what about the little girl? I know she isn't yours, but we can't just leave her here. Gabe, you can't burn the place down with her in it," Kari said puzzledly.

"The staff here is going to take her to family."

"Ju, I need you to get all the information off her phone and see what you come up with. Like I said before, she didn't come up with this shit alone. That last number that just called her, see what the connection is with the both of them."

"On it." Ju took the phone and headed out the door, and we followed behind him.

"I appreciate y'all for coming and helping me with this shit. She had a crew, so that shit would've been hard to execute by myself. I'm still not comfortable; it's something about all of this shit is still off. It took a little longer to get what we needed done, and Natalie tried to be hard, but this shit isn't her. She came at us as if she was acting alone, and her pops tried to back her up, but look at his as. As soon as he signed everything over to her, she killed his ass."

"Why though? Why would she go through all this with nobody here to back her shit up? That's some crazy ass shit. Like, she's dead and all the other people she involved is dead. All because they wanted control of the Carter Cartel?!" I was confused as fuck, but it's time to get to the bottom of this shit. We made it back to the Villa that Juelz rented for us, and everyone went to freshen up.

And just like that, we were back to ourselves like we hadn't just cleared a cartel. With how fast shit moved in our world, we almost had to run in order to keep up. I wouldn't have it any other way though.

"I'm hungry, I'm about to order some food. Do y'all want something?" Gabe asked, walking into the family room with some menus.

"Yeah, just order some fajitas, tacos, and quesadillas with all the fixings. I would just get enough for everyone," I told him.

"Count me out. I'm about to go change and see what the nightlife hitting for. Y'all asses talking about going to bed and shit. Nah, I'ma party before we get out of here in the morning." Mel was the wildest of the bunch, but we were all close. He was the opposite of his Nori in so many ways. Like now, Nori had his eyes on the tv smoking a blunt and was more than likely going to take his ass to bed after he ate. I'm not sure what the nigga was watching because the shit was in full Spanish with no damn subtitles. Last I checked the only language that nigga spoke was nigga.

"You better be damn careful out here. We're not with you, but if some shit seems off, call if you need us." I dapped him, and he headed upstairs to change his clothes.

"Oh shit! Lynx, I need to talk to you for a minute," JuJu said, getting everyone's attention.

"Son, is everything alright?" Juelz asked him.

"Umm... yes, and no. I need to talk this through with Lynx." He turned his attention to my brother as they both engaged in deep conversation. My phone beeped, and I got a text message from Bria.

Bri-Bri: I hope you're alright. I
haven't heard from you since you
left, and I wanted to make sure that
you were ok.

"Fuckkkkkk!" Lynx roared as he walked out on the patio, and I jumped to my feet to go see what was going on.

"What's up?" Nori and I both walked out to see what was up. Ju came walking out onto the patio with his laptop in hand, and I looked from him to Lynx.

"Is somebody gon' tell us what the fuck is going on?" I questioned, clearly irritated.

"Lynx was right; Natalie wasn't working alone. It seems that she was in a relationship with Kasharra Jones, and they both were seeing Romelo Carter. Natalie wanted a child, but she was unable to conceive, so Kasharra chose to have the baby, and the father of that child is Romelo Carter."

"The fuck are you saying! My fuckin' brother? My brother, nigga? That's the fuckin' rat?" Nori pulled his gun from his waist with tears in his eyes because this was some hard shit for us to hear!

"So, let me get this shit straight. Mel is the nigga that was recording us and leaking all of this shit to them?!" I was ready to kill this nigga straight the fuck up.

"Out of all the shit that we've done for this nigga, he bites the muthafuckin' hand that feeds him like this! That's our muthafuckin' blood! We trusted this nigga to do right by us! That's my aunt's son! That's your muthafuckin' brother!" He pointed at Nori, and my boy was just stoned faced. I knew this shit was taking him out.

"He's about to leave, I think we need to follow him to see where he leads us," I told them.

"Agreed. Ju, you need to take this ride with us. The rest of the family can stay behind; we got you protected. Nori, you know how I feel about a disloyal muthafucka. This shit for us is a little different because you my brother, through and through, and I know you didn't have shit to do with this. So, if that shit's in the back of your mind, erase it. When it comes to you and us, we know what it is. Believe that. Mel is your brother. I'ma let you make that call, but until then, let's keep this between us."

"I'm sorry, man. I didn't know anything about this. What the fuck! Do you know what this will do to my mom?! Fuck, man, fuck!!! This nigga was about to send me and the rest of y'all away for life! He had NO FUCKIN' REGARD for us! Fuck he had none for me as his fuckin' brother!" Nori roared, lifting the table and sending it over the patio. Just as he did that, Gabe was walking by. He looked out at us and swung the door open.

"What the hell wrong with his ass! Welp! There goes your incidental fee, Ju! This big muscle head ass nigga out there throwing furniture. They gon' stop renting to you drug dealers, that's why ion rent to they ass. I do a muthafuckin' drug dealer and thug screening on my Airbnb properties. Fuck that! Go sell drugs and kill niggas in your own shit," Gabe spat as he slammed the door. I shook my head because Lynx really needed to get his father in-law some damn help.

"He's leaving." JuJu pointed out, and we saw him talking to Kari. She gave him a hug, and he left out of the door.

"No worries, I just had Kari grab a tag out of my bag and put it on his clothes. That's the reason she hugged him. Let's go." He headed for the door, and Juelz nodded at Lynx, so I assumed he knew what the deal was from his calm demeanor. Nori followed the route that was on the map. The only thing we had to do was wait for him to get to where he was going. The ride was quiet because we all knew that we would eventually have to kill our own family. See what the fuck I mean? Right when you think shit sweet, you get hit with a right hook that shows your ass it's really sour. Mel, that man was our fucking family. I had so much respect for him, his mama, and his brother. They were all we fucking had growing up. A nigga would have done anything for Mel's ass. It was nothing in my mind to make me feel like he would do some shit like this to us. Now everything was making sense. This was the missing fucking piece. The reason why the IP addresses were connecting to us was because his ass was always with us! This shit probably had folks looking at my ass although Lynx knew better. Still! Fucking Mel? Mel? Nah, this shit right here, cut too fucking deep.

"Damn, it's a security gate!" Nori shook his head.

"Oh, give me a second. I was texting my wife goodnight." He chuckled. A few seconds later, the gate opened, and we headed to the location where he had stopped.

"The alarms and cameras are all shut down. We have an hour to do whatever it is we're doing." We all got out of the car and walked down to the house. We decided to go through the back of the house because we didn't know what to expect if we went through the front. It didn't take Nori no time to get us in, and the door led us into the kitchen area of the house. It was a pretty big house, so we had to maneuver through it, but we heard talking coming from one of the rooms with the light on.

"They killed her! That was your fuckin' daughter! You said you would protect them both, and your bitch ass failed! I can't even find Kasharra, and I don't even know what's up with my daughter. When I gave y'all the fuckin videos, you should have just sent that shit to the Feds. I would have automatically gotten his operation. These niggas were definitely going to get the chair or spend the rest of their lives in jail!

But no, yo' bitch ass wanted to see my pussy ass cousin crawling on his knees. You're lucky I got a little collateral back home just in case we need it, but I want my muthafuckin' money and I want that shit now. If they ever find out it's me, they're going to kill me!" Mel spoke loud and clear.

"So, you just sat there and watched them torture our daughter?" Some woman questioned.

"Bitch, did you come and help out when I called y'all to tell you we were going onto the compound?! Stupid hoe, it should've been your ass instead of Nat!" Mel spat.

"Enough! You had one fucking job! You don't get shit until I got Lynx Carter's head on the chopping block!" That voice was all too familiar, and now we know why he was calling Natalie.

"I guess we'll have to see whose head will make it there first, bitch!" Lynx said, easing into the room with both of his guns pointed at them. They all reached for their guns, but it was too late; we had the drop on them. Mel dropped his head, and Nori gave that nigga no time to explain. He started beating his fuckin' ass and I didn't blame him. I was ready to let off in his pussy ass. It's the fact that this nigga just said fuck us and everything we stand for. Yeah, if Nori can't do it, best believe I'ma make this pussy muthafucka eat these bullets.

"I didn't think you were smart enough to figure out it was me. I underestimated you, so what do we do now, because I can still get that video to the authorities?" He shrugged.

"You killed my daughter, you stupid fuck!" Lynx held his gun out and let off multiple shots into Natalie's mom, with his attention still trained on Hector.

"I knew something was up with you, and it's that muthafuckin' greed. You should've taken your retirement money he left you and retired, nigga. Then to find out your nothing ass been fucking this money hungry hoe for years, and Nat is your daughter. Alonzo was a damn fool, because ain't no way he didn't know. Your ass would've been dead. Why come for me and mine?! You getting this nigga to help you was genius. I gotta give you credit for that. What I don't understand is why the fuck are you bothered with the Kassom family? I guess I can figure out why you decided to try me, but why them?" Lynx asked him.

"Juelz Kassom is a bitch made nigga! He's trash, and my beef with him is from years ago when he killed my brothers the night, they kidnapped his daughter. I couldn't figure it out for years, but I vowed never to stop until I found the person who killed them. He was untouchable and very hard to get to, so I had to wait him out. For years, I waited for my time to get our revenge. When I found out that you were connected to them and were a part of his organization, that sealed the deal for me." He smiled, but that shit was cut short when a bullet pierced his chest. We all turned to look in the direction that the shot came from, and it was JuJu's ass.

"Arghhhhhh!" Hector cried out in pain from the shot as he dropped to his knees.

"Let me find out this nigga got the sauce!" I blurted.

"That's for my fuckin' dad!" He turned his phone around, and Juelz was on FaceTime. This fuckin' family was solid as fuck! Damn! Lynx decided to cut this short, and I was surprised because he's into making a nigga suffer.

Nori pulled his Machete, handed it to Lynx, and this nigga went straight into that nigga Hector's throat, killing him instantly!

"Y'all gotta let me explain. I was in need of the money, and I just couldn't pass up his offer. You niggas always left me out and acted as if I was just some secondhand worker. You didn't treat this nigga that way! You always treated him better than me! Y'all was always sending for him to go on trips and making sure his pockets were always laced! Putting him in a position to make millions!

I tried to stay loyal to you niggas, but y'all made that shit hard. But you not gon' kill me, 'cause I got a lil' package you gon' want back, my nigga. It was just something in me that felt like shit could go wrong. Now you gon' get me the money I need, let me walk up out of here, and you'll get your kid back." He smirked, and Lynx lost his mind!

"You touched my fuckin' son, nigga! My fuckin' son, nigga!" he beat that nigga bloody, but he didn't kill him. I have never in my life seen my brother like this. I was ready to kill this nigga. He touched my nephew, and he knows that's off limits. Lynx was immediately on his phone; I'm assuming he was calling Malayah.

"Hello." Her voice came through the speaker.

"Layah, where is Brayden?" He asked her.

"He's with Aunt Nae. She's been asking for him, so I took him over there this morning, why?" She questioned.

"I call you back." He ended the call and dialed another number.

"Hey, baby." Aunt Nae's voice came through the speaker. It was late, so I'm sure she was asleep.

"Ma, where is Bray?" He asked her.

"He's in the room sleep. Tianna put him in the bed for me before she left," she said, and that had us all puzzled.

"Tianna!" Lynx yelled.

"Why was she there?" He asked her.

"She said she was stopping by to check on me. When she saw that Brayden was here, she got pizza. I had a headache and needed to lay down, so she fed him and then put him to bed," she explained.

"What's wrong?" She asked.

"Ma, go check on Brayden. Go now, Ma!" He yelled, and I'm sure that scared her.

"I'm going now." You could hear her moving around the room.

"Oh my God! He's not here! What is going on? Oh my God! Where is he, Lynx!" Lynx hung up the phone without responding. Then Nori did what the fuck he had to do, and that was empty the muthafuckin' clip!

"What the fuck, man! Why these niggas want to fuck with me! We gotta get back to the States, but we may not make it in time!" Lynx was on go, but he was right. We're not sure what the fuck was up with Tianna.

"Why would she even let Mel get her involved with this shit?" Nori said, not believing that it was Tianna. She was Lynx's assistant, who did everything from booking trips to making deals on our cars and houses. Damn, you can't trust no fuckin' body these days.

CHAPTER 16
Lynx

I was ready to tear this jet up. We couldn't get there fast enough, and I needed to be on the ground in New York right fuckin' now! Thank God I had a team guarding my wife, and they're on their way to Tianna's place. If this bitch does anything to my son, the amount of fury I'm going to bring down on her is indescribable.

We were all on edge and running off adrenaline at this point. I was trying to hold it together, but I felt like I was hanging off a cliff by a rope. I tried weighing the whole structure of events. I thought I'd done the right thing by putting my family closest to me to make some money but to see that Mel would even fucking play like this? With my son? My child? The one thing in the world I would kill God himself about? What the fuck?

My cousin and my fuckin' assistant! Two people that knew

every fuckin' thing down to what time I took a shit. I felt so fuckin' weak. So, defeated. My heart was hammering, and my breathing ragged. I had to have my child. I swear on life I couldn't live without him.

"How long are they saying before we get on the ground?" Gabe asked while his leg jumped up and down.

"Another hour," Malik advised him.

"Shit! That pilot needs to speed this shit up. Every second that crazy bitch has my grandson is a second too long!" He spat. My phone started ringing, and it was Malayah calling me on FaceTime.

"Hey, baby." I rubbed my hands over my face.

"Lynx, do you know anything? I need my son! How could you let this happen?! I need my baby! Please get my baby!" She cried as Gia came to the phone.

"I got her. Y'all just bring my grandson home." She hung up, and I lost my mind. I've never hurt or cried over anything other than my mother dying, but this shit broke me. He's an innocent child, and to think you can come in and harm him is some bitch made shit. And bitch or not, that bitch gon' have to see me. Which is why I told them if they found her, I wanted her untouched. It was the longest hour, but we were finally on the ground. Kari and Jah's plane had just landed as well, but I couldn't wait for them. We had to go.

"Mr. Carter, she wasn't at the address that we checked nor was she at her mother's house," Tony said to me as we headed to my truck.

"Lynx! We got her!" Gabe yelled out as they jumped into

the trucks and sped off. We sped out behind them, and I prayed my boy was alright. Thirty minutes later, we were pulling up to this warehouse.

"What the hell is going on? Who the hell lives here? This house is crazy as fuck!" Malik stated. When I looked over at Nori, he was just out of it. I know his mind was on his brother, but fuck that nigga. The way he did us, he's lucky we didn't do him dirty. We pulled to the back of the grounds and got out.

"What's up?" I asked when we all got out of the cars.

"We look out for our own. That's you and Malayah's son and Gabe's grandson. He never wants to see his daughter in that kind of pain, and he loves his grandson. She wasn't hard to find. Mel rented a new apartment, and we found her there," Juelz said to me, and we walked inside the building that was in the back of the house. I was taken aback seeing all of the women from the family inside and my wife fucking Tianna up.

"You took my baby bitch all because your hoe ass was jealous! You wanted my fuckin' husband! You hoes always want something you can't have!" *Whap! Whap!*

Malayah was just on the phone crying, and now her ass was in full on beat a bitch mode. I was starting to get whiplash from how fast all this shit was happening, but my heart was relieved as fuck.

"Yessss, hunny! Tear dat ass up! GBC, baby! We outchea! Pour a lil' of that ponent stuff on her, Toya!" Ms. Lai instructed while she and Aunt Cynt sat in some chairs, smoking blunts and egging shit on. This was a whole fucking show. What the fuck? I have never in my life seen no shit like this. All the guys just stood around and watched, so I decided to sit this one out and let my wife have the show.

"Pleaseee! I didn't know why he wanted me to take him. I'm sorry! Lynnnxxxx, please help me! I love you! I swear I didn't mean for this to go so far. You didn't want me, but I thought that one day you would change your mind. When you married her, I knew there was no chance for me, so I got with Mel. I didn't know that he was dealing with Natalie and Kasharra."

"I didn't even know about his daughter until recently. Pleasseee help me! I wasn't going to hurt him. He just asked me to get him and take him to my house!" She cried, and Gia let off a shot into her arms and her legs. She hit the ground screaming in pain. Two people in hazmat suits walked in with a container, and all the guys stepped the fuck back, but I stepped closer because this definitely piqued my interest. I didn't notice it before, but all of the damn ladies had on t-shirts that read *Baby Snatchin' Bitches Get Put In Ditches!* I had to chuckle because what the hell was going on? I pulled up a seat and sat down with the ladies.

"Can we go to the zoo now?" Ciera asked, and I swear I wouldn't have ever thought that sweet lady was gangsta like that. I've never seen any of them in this light. When they say they ride for each other, that's what it is. When the guys opened the box, snakes started crawling out of the box. The guys lifted Tianna up and placed her inside as she cried out for God, her mom, and for me to help her. But I felt nothing.

At one point, I had love for her as a friend. She tried to

come for me once, but I put an end to that shit quickly. She worked with me too closely, and I only wanted a business relationship.

Seeing the snakes bite her on every part of her body was some shit I thought I'd never witness before, and I wanted to add that shit to my line up. This shit gave a whole new meaning to the phrase, snake a nigga.

"I like you, nephew! You didn't even flinch! That's what the fuck I'm talkin' about! A real boss! Them niggas over there scared! Look at they ass by the door!" Ms. Lai laughed, and she was right. I turned, and Gabe's ass was sitting on the table Indian style, and the rest of them were towards the back.

"A boss and a fine one at that. Nephew, you alright with me. Any time you need to put us on your payroll, you just give us a call. We're up there in age, and they try to make us stay back, but as you can see, we still got it. Ain't that right, Lai?" Ms. Cynt smiled, while she smoked her blunt. Once they got her in the box with the snakes, they closed the lid and carried her out. She'll be dead by the time they get her to the zoo. Before Malayah could make it outside, I pulled her to the side.

"Where is Bray?"

"For the sake of our son, you need to come out of this shit! Look at everything that's happened in the last fuckin' month, Lynx!"

"I asked you a question, where is my son?!" I gritted. I was trying to be patient with her, but that shit was hard to do.

"He's in the house!"

"I know we have a lot to work through, and I'ma do that

shit because my family is worth the fight. But you need to kill this fuckin' attitude! I love you. You know why I made the moves I did. Stop acting like that. When this is over, I'm going back to Puerto Rico, and I want you and my son to come back with me. I know you're mad, but be mad at me in our home." She rolled her eyes at me and walked off.

I walked out to join the rest of the crew. Tianna was now in a cage, and it was hanging over the water.

"Grandson, we had enough fun. Come on and hit the damn button so I can go to bed," she said to me. Walking over to the machine, I guided the cage into the water. Tianna wasn't moving, so it's possible that she was already dead.

Once the cage was underwater, we walked back to the main house. I wanted to get my son and head over to my in-law's house. I needed some much-needed rest; I think we all did. Today's events were enough to last us all a lifetime. I didn't realize I had so many snakes in my camp, but I'm so glad we cleared that shit up. Now it was time to focus on my family and get the love of my life back home in my arms. It's going to be a task because she's stubborn as hell, but I'm going to get her back.

Once we made it to the house, I spent some time with Brayden. I needed that time with my son, because I was still in my feelings about what happened to him. My aunt Nae has been calling nonstop, apologizing. If something had happened to my son, I honestly don't know how I would've reacted. Having my kid changed me in so many ways. I believe it made me a better man. I've never loved a human being as much as I love my kid.

It's a different kind of love, for sure. I feel the same way about my wife. When I feel like my life is being altered or my family is under attack, my mindset changes.

After making sure he was sound asleep, I eased out of his bed and left the room. Layah was still up watching television, trying to act like she didn't notice me standing here. Her and this damn attitude was pissing me off. Leaning against the door, I just stood and watched her for a minute. We'd been through all this shit today, and her ass still wanted to be mad. Some women can do the most and my damn wife is one of them.

"So, are you just gonna ignore me and act as if I'm not standing here?"

"I see you, but I'm not sure why you're standing there. Like why are you even here? My son was kidnapped because of your bullshit! All because you can't keep your enemies in check! On top of all that, your family member is the one that did the shit! So, I see you, but I don't have shit to say to you! He could have been killed, Lynx!" She spat. The disrespect coming from this woman has me on fire.

Malayah and I have never argued like this, and we damn sure haven't been at odds like this since being married. I was in her face, pulling her ass from the bed within seconds.

"Before you open your fuckin' mouth and talk to me like that again, let's get some shit straight. Don't ever disrespect me! EVER! I feel like I been telling yo' ass that way too much lately. I be trying my hardest not to go off on yo' ass, but you keep on pushing it! Yes, it was my disloyal ass cousin that did the shit! Hell, he's the one that started it all, but that was some shit that wasn't in my control. I didn't know the dude hated me that bad.

He wanted my spot, and it takes a lot to get in my spot. These niggas out here let greed get the best of them. Layah, I have never disrespected you. Please stop doing that shit with me. I don't have to repeat why I made my decisions because you know why.

I will come for anybody that threatens my livelihood. I married you because I wanted that shit with you, lil mama. You came up with this insane ass conclusion that I didn't care about your feelings. The fuck is wrong with you! All the love I have in me from the depths of my soul, is for you. My first thought of the day is of you and my son. No other woman can ever give me what you have given me.

The time I spent away from you, I was still true to you. I wish I would let that dirty bitch get on my dick; I slept in a separate bedroom. At the end of the day, I did all of this, not just for me and my family, but for you and yours. And this is how you treat me? You got that shit, baby girl. I'm going back to Puerto Rico. When you really want to talk, I guess you'll come home."

Moving to the door quickly, I accidentally knocked her purse onto the floor. Some of her things fell out, and something caught my eye. Bending down to pick it up, I couldn't believe what the fuck I was holding.

"Are these yours?" I asked confused as fuck! I was ready to explode on her ass, is this girl fuckin' serious!" By the look in

165

her eyes, I knew the answer to that shit, but I still wanted to hear her say it.

"Answer me dammit!" I roared, and she jumped with tears in her eyes.

"Yes! They're mine."

"The fuck! I thought we talked about this! You said you wanted to have another baby? And even if you didn't want another kid right now, why fuckin' lie about it and go behind my back to take birth control?!" I was pissed!

"I just felt like having a baby wasn't the time for us. You were already not spending enough time at home. Yes, we have a nanny to help out, but I needed you active," she tried to explain.

"You fuckin' lied to me! One thing I hate the most is a liar! I would have respected you just being honest." I turned to walk off, and she tried to stop me.

"Don't fuckin' touch me!" I left the room, because I knew if I stayed, things would only get worse. Lying to me is like stabbing a nigga in the back. Now I'm not sure if I can trust you. I'm exhausted as hell, but going back to Puerto Rico is the best thing to do.

CHAPTER 17

Malayah

A few days have passed, and I'm still trying to wrap my mind around all that's happened. Getting the call from Lynx about Brayden and then later finding out that someone had taken my son damn near suffocated me. I was such a complete mess I didn't know what to do. Lynx and I are not in a good place. Our son being taken only made matters worse. Not to mention him finding out about me taking birth control.

I'll never say that I don't love my husband, because I do. I also know how much he loves me. In my eyes, I just don't think he's adjusted to being married and having a family. He says he wants this life with us, but he doesn't demonstrate that all the time. I've toggled back and forth about the divorce I filed a month ago. I haven't heard anything from Zayah about the progress of the divorce filing. I've called her several times, but have yet to hear back from her. Picking up my phone, I dialed her number.

"Hey, babe. How are you?" Her perky voice came blaring through the speaker.

"I'm doing alright. I haven't heard from you in a while and just wanted to see if you had any updates?" I sighed.

"I haven't heard anything. They're still saying the courts are working on cases from mid-July still. I'm sorry, babe. Layah, are you really sure you want to do this? Prior to the bullshit, you were so happy and in love. I mean, I know there were minor issues, but nothing to make you run down to divorce court over. It's hard as fuck out here living the single life, trying to find the right damn man. I've come to terms with the fact that I'm going to grow old and alone, but you have a man that loves you!

Put some demands on his ass and sit your married ass down. He's faithful to you, and he treats you amazingly. I know you love him, stop acting like that. Keep on, and some lil' hoe gon' be in your bed, calling your home her home, calling your man her man, and Bray calling her step mommy." I hit the FaceTime button because now her ass was tripping. She picked up laughing.

"Bitch! Don't push it!" I laughed with her. Zayah was such a beautiful girl. She had it all. A vibrant career, she's rich, beautiful, and OMG her body was something I wish I had. She was a thick woman. Some would consider her BBW, but when I tell you baby girl was fya, believe me when I say she's fya! I loved my friend to death. Her and Bri were my riders for sure. Zayah and

I met in law school, instantly hit it off, and we've been rocking ever since.

"Stop with all of that growing old and alone shit too! You're beautiful, finnneee as hell. 'Cause these niccas is always trying to get your ass! Trust me, somebody's son would be blessed to have you. As for me and mine, ion know! Sometimes I want to mop the floor with his fine gun totin' ass, and others, I wanna ride the dick 'til the sun comes up. He just doesn't have his priorities in order enough for me. He's responsible, loves me and Bray, and takes care of me mentally and sexually when he's there. That's the biggest part of what I mean by priorities," I told her.

"Layah, baby, that's not a normal man you're talking about. You knew being married to a man like him wasn't going to be easy. You knew what kind of profession he was in before you agreed to stay married to him. Your marriage was very unique, but even in its uniqueness, you two were made for each other. I'm a divorce attorney, and I've assisted in so many families breaking up that it's hard as fuck watching and going through it sometimes. My parents, and yours, have had long-lasting marriages, and don't think for one second there wasn't trials in it. It's hard work, but they stayed true to their vows. I think you really need to talk to Lynx, spend some quality time together, and try to work this out. He's worth it, boo thang. Aren't you guys going on vacation soon for your birthday?" I heard what she was saying, and I would definitely think about it.

"We are, but he isn't going. I haven't mentioned it again to him at all. He's mad at me, so he hasn't called me in a couple of days. I just want a break from it all; I need it without all of the stresses of life. So, I'm going with my parents and the rest of the family. You should come with us, Za-Za! It will be fun, and it's for my birthday," I urged, hoping she would come.

"Girl, I have toooo many cases to get done and an upcoming hearing I need to prepare for."

"You can prepare on vacation on your downtime. I have a case coming up myself, and I can bet you my ass is going to be on those beaches in Belize soaking in the sun and drinking as many tequila sunrises as I can. You never know your husband could be on that damn island! Besides all that, you get to spend a week with my dad, and we know how much you love him." I rolled my eyes, and she burst out laughing.

"Don't do that! Don't be a hater all your life. That man's is so damn funny and adorable. I told Ma Gia she's so lucky." She smiled.

"Ewwwww, I don't know why y'all think my dad is so cute. Anyhoo, you should come, even if it's just for a few days. I tried to get Bria to come, but she's emotionally not there right now." I gave a half smile.

"Yeah, I talked to her last night briefly. I'm praying for both of them. But look, I have to go. When are you guys leaving?" She asked, and that gave me hope that she would join us. Zayah is a bag of fun, baby, and always the life of the party. That's why her and my daddy got along so good.

"We leave on Friday." I smiled because I knew her ass was about to start cursing.

"Bitch! That's in two damn days! Send me all of the information, and I'll let you know tonight. Do I need to get my own place or is it room in the house for me?" She questioned.

"Plenty of room." We spoke for a few more minutes with promises of speaking later tonight. I went downstairs, and my mom was cooking dinner.

"Hey, mom. Do you need some help?" I asked, popping a fry in my mouth.

"No, it's almost done. I just had to make some onion rings and fries. Ms. Nadine called to check on you and Brayden today. Layah, sit down so we can talk."

I wanted to do everything but talk. The way the kitchen smelled had my stomach growling, and I would rather be stuffing my face than be listening to my mom preach about what was going on with my out-of-order ass life. Still, I sat my ass down and listened to what she had to say.

My mom checked the food once more, wiped her island, and then propped her hand on her hip. I knew then she was about to give me a mouthful.

"I'm a little disappointed in you. I know you love your child; hell, I was just as angry about Bray being missing. Now stop treating his family like that. Those people love you and that little boy. We have had plenty of bullshit going on in this family that could last us a lifetime. You need to get out of your feelings and go talk to your husband. Your dad and I will keep Brayden if you want to take a trip with just you and your husband." She smiled.

"Gia, why the hell you keep on volunteering our damn services? Thing 1 and thing 2 need to take they ass home. They done overstayed they welcome! They ass been squatting for too damn long. You know there are laws for squatting. If they stay too damn long, they can claim our shit! And she's a lawyer! She can take it right from under our nose! It's always that second child that do you wrong. I already know her lil' chimpanzee ass gon' put me in a nursing home!" My dad went on and on.

"You got that right. I'ma take all your money and leave you old ass broke." I laughed, and that straightened him right on up.

"That's why I was on FaceTime with Lynx, and I saw some chick in the back making him eggs and bacon. I think she was wearing your robe too. They probably about to go on a date on his G6. You know what they say about a rich nigga with a G6 and a fine bit-"

"Gabriel Thomas! Shut your ass up and go watch your grandson while he's outside playing!" I wanted to throw this damn apple I was eating at the back of his head for playing with me about my damn husband. That's still a sensitive situation.

I walked out to see what Bray was doing. My dad was lying on the couch, and Brayden came running into the house. I'm surprised he left the patio door open for him. His ass probably didn't want to get up and check on him. My parents had a little play area built for the kids right outside the patio door. They also gated the pool off, which was a good idea.

"Pop-Pop! Here my snake-snake." Brayden clapped, handing his snake to my dad. He saw that damn rubber snake in the store and cried to have it, so I got it for him. "Damn, they sure make these damn things look real as hell." The moment my dad said that shit, I saw the damn snake moving. Then he opened his mouth wide as shit, looking straight at my dad.

"Ahhhhh, hell nawl! I know you fuckin' lyin'! Giaaaaaa, helppppp!" He slung that damn snake so hard it bounced on the wall and back on his ass. I was breaking my ass trying to get my damn baby out of the way. My mom came running into the family room, and my dad climbed to the top of the bar with his fire gun in hand.

"Gabe! Get the hell down and get that thing out of here! Oh, shit! That's a big ass snake. How the hell did it get in here?" My mom asked, looking at my dad.

"The damn Omen! That's how it got in here, and now that nigga wanna curl up and go the fuck to sleep. Mmmmm, mmmmm, Gia gon' and get it out of here 'cause if you don't, you gonna be less a family room," he exclaimed.

"And yo' ass gonna be sleeping in the guest bedroom for a month. Get that shit out of my house, Gabriel Thomas, before that shit bites my grandson!" My mom fussed.

"That lil' cradle from the grave nigga the one who brought it in here! I think his lil' ass should take him the fuck back! My motto is you go the same way the hell came!" He fussed, pulling out his phone.

"Hello." Uncle Truth's voice came through the speaker.

"Tru, I need you to come over here. It's about three big black niggas and a big burly bitch in my house with guns! Hurry 'cause I don't wanna get bit, I mean, die!" I stood in the doorway safely away from the snake, laughing at his big, overgrown ass trying to get Uncle Truth over here to get that snake out of the house. This man was nuts!

My mom called Uncle Truth and told him what was in the house and not to come. It took my dad all day to get that damn snake out of the house. Yeah, it was definitely time for a vacation.

A couple days later, we were at the airport and on our way to Belize. I didn't want to ask Lynx for the plane. A part of me wanted to do things the normal way. See, things like this is when my marriage hit the hardest. Private planes and just all-out VIP services. My husband had set the tone these last few years, but it wasn't enough to make me bend. I really wanted to do something different from our normal life, so I decided to take a commercial flight. I talked my dad and mom into traveling on Delta Airlines with me. They both put up a fight because they were so accustomed to flying private, but they did it for me. I decided to go to Belize and would travel to Bali before the year was over.

We finally boarded our flight, and my dad started acting up immediately.

"I have flown commercial before, and I don't remember these damn planes being this small. I feel like me and the damn next person gon' be boxed in together like a damn two-piece meal at damn KFC. Mmmmm, mmmm, and why the hell you didn't get us first class seats? I feel like your hateful ass is trying to be funny. I'ma tell you what's gonna be real funny, if we get to Belize and they cancel our Airbnb. How the hell are you able to ball out at Chanel, Louis, and YSL, but we in these tight ass seats? For what you spent on looks, yo' ass could have BOOKED a jet.

You got yo' damn priorities fucked all the way up. Big headed ass. Trying to do shit for the Gram, but we on Soul Plane!" He fussed, and I shook my head. When I booked our flights, Dad surprised me and said he was getting the house for everyone, and I was so damn excited. I didn't trust his ass, so he showed me the house online, and it was beautiful. Despite my dad complaining the entire time, boarding was complete, and it was almost time to go. I low key was ready to get off this damn plane, and we had just gotten on.

"I know what the hell I saw, and that woman ain't real! I don't know what it is, but it ain't human! And I know a human when I see it, and her ass ain't it!" Some lady yelled, and that caused us all to turn around.

"See this that shit right here! Gia, what the hell she talking about? Who ain't real?" My dad started looking from me to Mom and then around the plane.

"I want off! Y'all can stay on this damn plane, but I bet y'all asses won't get off!" She yelled, trying to make her way up front.

"Who won't get off! Hell to the nawl! We all know when a black person says they done seen some shit, that means they done seen some shit. Her ass looks a lil' slow and crazy, but I'm with her on this one. Y'all asses seen Final Destination! Fuck that! Death can stay where the hell it's at. I'm not trying to go ring the doorbell to the pearly gates just to have my ass dropped back down to Lucifer's doorsteps instead.

They already got this lil' nigga, they don't need my ass. I'm too saved, sanctified, and filled with the holy ghost! Hell to the no! If that crazy heifer right there said she ain't real, her ass ain't real! Give us our money back, and let me take my ass over to private side so I can get me a damn plane. Gia, if you and your daughter coming, I suggest y'all get the hell up. I can't ride all the way to Belize knowing a woman with no head is back there plotting to take us the hell out!" I dropped my head because this man was serious as hell and had people on the plane agreeing with him too.

It was a line of them trying to get off the plane, and the crazy lady that started this shit was at the front. Delta hadn't closed the doors, so they let us off, and a couple hours later, we were on a private jet that my dad rented to get us over to Belize. We were delayed, but about four hours later, we were in Belize, and I was so excited. My dad and mom fussed the entire trip about how he showed his ass. He doesn't know, but I recorded the whole thing and plan to show the family as soon as they all get there. When we pulled up to the house, my mouth was on the floor. This place was beautiful.

"Dad, this doesn't look like the house you showed me online," I declared as we pulled up to the security gate.

"I changed it. I wanted to go all out for my baby girl's birthday." He smiled, and I was so excited I jumped up from the backseat and wrapped my arms around his neck.

"Thank you, Dad!" The moment we pulled in front of the house, my damn smile turned to a frown, and I smacked the hell out of the back of my dad's head. "Hit me again, and you gon' be walking around with a damn nub. Now get yo' ass out of this car and act like you got some sense. Every time God blesses yo' ungrateful ass, you always blocking them same blessings. Now this billionaire ass husband of yours is still fighting for your ungrateful ass. Get out the car right now, and take Satan with you!" I started to argue with his ass, but my mom gave me the 'don't fuck with us' look.

When I got out of the car, Lynx and Nori were standing on the steps. I didn't expect to see him, but I guess it's time to talk to him. I had no more fight in me. It was my birthday trip, and I was on a beautiful island with the people I loved and adored. I was ready to slay and sip tropical drinks and see tropical views.

Before I made it up the steps, a few more SUV'S pulled up, and I got too excited when Zayah got out of the truck.

"Let's get this party started, boo!" She gyrated her body, and I knew it was about to be a good time. My girl was in travel gear but still looking fabulous. The high-waisted floral leggings she wore had her hips looking amazing, and the matching off the shoulder top that was tied in a knot under her breasts showed how even though her body was plus size, she was pressure. Zayah removed her oversized frames and tossed her long Bohemian knotless braids behind her back. When she noticed my parents, she ran over to them to greet them, and I walked up to my husband.

"Why didn't you tell me you were coming?" I asked him.

I was still pissed at him, but my man was so fine in his teal shorts, white tee, and Hermes slides. He was simple but still looked damn good. That was Lynx, though. He could make a Walmart shirt look amazing.

"Why didn't you invite me?" He shrugged, pulling me into him.

"Whatever." I flagged him off.

"We have a lot of things to work through, and I'm willing to work through them and fight for my wife and marriage. As a man, that's what I'm supposed to do. I'm never leaving you. If you want shit to change, we both are going to have to make some changes in this relationship. I'm mad as fuck that you lied to me, because you don't ever have to lie to me. If it's something you don't want to do, then don't do it.

We won't dig too deep right now, but by the time this vacation is over, everything that we need to talk about will be talked about. Oh yeah, this house is your house. Happy Birthday, beautiful lady!" He smiled, and he had my ass stuck on damn stupid.

"My house? You bought this for me! Oh, my fucking God! Lynx, thank you so much!" I screamed, jumping up and down. I couldn't believe that he purchased this house for me.

"Yessss, this is a beautiful house, and I love the real life statues they have in here as a part of the décor, hunny!" Grandma Lai said as she started touching all on Nori's body.

"Keep on, and I swear I'm telling Pop on yo' old ass. That nigga is young, and in his prime, there ain't shit you can do for him," my dad told her, and we were all laughing.

"I don't give a damn what you tell him. I can look at this fine ass man if I want to. Lawd, we always looking for a new president for the Fine Nigga Committee. Boy, you should tell yo' momma thank you every time you see her. 'Cause baby, you fine as hell!" Grams went on and on.

"You ain't never lied. That's a tree any woman would love to climb." Zayah tried to whisper that shit, but we all heard her, and so did Nori.

"Your room or mine?" He winked at her and walked into the bar area where the guys had started drinking.

"Wheeww, did he just... Girl, you betta go hop on that thang 'cause it looks like it was definitely thangin'!" Grams fell out laughing.

"My God, that man is beautiful. Who the hell is that?" Za questioned, and we were still in a fit of laughter. 'Cause, baby, Nori ass done ruffled some feathers. We settled in and relaxed until it was time for dinner. I couldn't wait for Kari and Laila to get here. This week is going to be so much fun.

A few hours later, it was time for dinner, and to my surprise, Lynx had a dinner for two set up down at the beach. The rest of the family decided they wanted to go out for dinner and give us some time alone.

I had to be honest with myself; I really love my husband and can't see my life without him. I apologized to him for being stubborn, but I had to stand my ground on talking to me about all decisions before he just makes them. That was something that we could have talked through. You never know, I may have had a better solution for all of us. This entire ordeal had me emotionally fucked up, because I thought I was losing my husband, and some bitch was threatening to turn over evidence she had on us. That's some crazy shit, and trust me, I understood what he was trying to do.

"Baby, I owe you an apology. I'm so sorry for the way I treated you and for not being honest about the birth control."

"Malayah, I love you and there is nothing more that I want in my life than to spend it with you. Just know when we have important discussions like that, I need the truth. I want you to have all my babies, but if that's not what you want, then we need to talk about it.

I sat there in amazement and couldn't believe my sight. There were candles and bouquets of red roses all around us, and the dinner table sat in the middle. It was breathtaking, and I loved the hell out of this man.

"I love you, and I'm sorry for almost divorcing you." I smiled, and we both burst out laughing.

"Girl, I was never letting that sit happen, especially with a father in-law like mine. Your dad and Zayah were stalling you in hopes that you would change your mind." He laughed, and I was sitting here in shock. I'ma fuck Zayah ass up.

"That's messed up! What if I really wanted that divorce?" I looked over at him.

"You didn't." He smiled, and we sat and ate our dinner. The steak and lobster we had for dinner was damn good, and now I was stuffed.

"This moment felt so good and right. I missed the fuck out of you, and I'm not gon' even bullshit you. I need to make love, fuck, and bust yo' ass down all night. It's been a minute; I need that shit now!" He stood from his seat quick as hell, lifting me from my seat. I was laughing so damn hard that I felt dizzy.

It took us no time to make it back to the house and into our bedroom. *Say It* by Usher came through the speakers. His tongue grazed my lips, and I pulled his bottom lip into my mouth and sucked the hell out of it. I was hungry as hell for this man. His fingers moved between my thighs as he started rubbing my clit. That shit had me trembling. Spreading my legs apart, he slid his dick back and forth, and all I could do was cry out the moment he eased inside of me.

"Oh my God!" I cried out as my body began to shake.

"Let me have my way tonight!" He growled into my ear.

"Ohhh shit, baby!" I cried with every thrust.

"Fuck! This pussy so fuckin' good!" He gritted, thrusting deep into me, and there wasn't shit I could do about it.

"Fuck me, baby!" I demanded.

"Come ride this dick, baby!" He pulled out of me and sat on the bed. Then I eased down on him, bouncing and rocking my body back and forth on his shit. He gripped my ass cheeks, spreading them apart, and started pounding the shit out of my walls.

"Ahhh, shit! I'm cumming! I love you!" I screamed out, which fueled him to take this to another level. His strokes were so deep I could feel that shit in my chest.

"Urgghhhhhh!" He roared, releasing into me so hard that shit shook me.

"You know I love you. There is nothing that I won't do for you." He kissed me on my lips and pulled me up for a shower.

CHAPTER 18
Lynx

Four Months Later

T
hings have been hectic with my family since all that shit went down with Mel. We told my auntie that Mel got himself in a situation and was ultimately killed. There was no way that we could tell her that Nori killed him and did that shit with good reason. She had been keeping her distance and has not been herself ever since. I knew she was hurt; any mother would be hurt to lose a child. I'm a father, and when I thought my son was gone, I was ready to join him. However, her pain would heal. Mel was where he needed to be. He had to pay the price for his actions.

I'm still trying to wrap my mind around the fact that Mel would even stoop so fuckin' low to do us like that. I know money makes you do some stupid ass shit, but damn, he could've come to me. I would've given him anything! My damn last, if I had to. I've always been that person to have all my family covered if they needed me, and to know that pussy nigga played with me like that makes me want to kill his ass all over again. I do feel bad for my aunt because she's heartbroken about the nigga.

I can also tell that Nori is really fighting his demons over that shit. He loved the fuck out of his brother. They were so close, so I knew hearing him talk shit about setting us up and wanting us in jail fucked him up. That shit definitely did a number on me, but the moment I realized that his bitch ass tried to put us all under the jail, it was fuck that nigga, and I wanted his ass dead. Cousin or not, he had to die. I hope Nori can find some peace with all that's happened.

"Hey, babe. When do you leave for Cuba?" Malayah asked, jolting me from my thoughts.

Ever since our time in Belize, we have really been taking time with each other. I don't care what nobody says, fucking the love of your life on an island was some next-level shit. I mean, we technically lived in the tropics, but Belize was magical. Shit got us where we needed to be. It took some time for me to realize that I really had to listen and understand how she was really feeling. I never want my family to think that I'm not there for them when they need me. I will admit that it was hard adjusting to having a wife at home when we first got married. I was used to coming and going as I pleased. All that being considerate of the hours I kept, spending time, and checking in wasn't really me, but knowing that those three things kept my wife happy had me having my ass at home at 8 p.m. sharp. She was tossing out the pussy like a Frisbee too.

"In a few days. Is everything alright?"

"Yeah, I forgot the dates. I need to make sure I'm home at a decent time with Bray, that's all. You know I have closing arguments starting next week, so I have to start prepping for it." She smiled, and all I could do was look at her. She's sitting here with a messy bun in her hair, with her glasses sitting on the bridge of her nose, and I found that shit so sexy.

"Do you need me to stay home and help with him?" She looked over at me as if something was wrong.

"No, I'm alright. I talked to Aunt Nae yesterday and she might come down to visit next week. With her and Camille here, I think I'll be good."

The doorbell sounded off, and I knew it was Malik. He had called me earlier saying he was on his way over. He and Bria are still going through it, but I'm hoping they can find a way through it. I know he's pissed with her, but if she's trying to talk to him, maybe he needs to hear her out. She called me several times about him still not speaking to her. If he does say something, it's regarding the house or her car, but nothing about the relationship. When I made it downstairs, he was already in the family room.

"Sup." I dapped him up.

"Nothing much, man. Just trying to take it day by day." He looked lost. I could understand how he was feeling because hell, I was in the same damn boat with my wife. Now things are good, and I'm happy as fuck that things are back to normal.

"Bro, I want to talk to you about something." He walked over to the bar to pour him a drink.

"What's up?" I asked, taking a seat at the bar.

Just looking at my brother, I couldn't help but smile internally. I remember when we were young, dusty-ass kids just talking about the shit we have today. Malik grew up to be everything we envisioned. I loved my brother to death. Just thinking about how Mel had not only betrayed us but his brother too, had me feeling blessed that God gave me a solid-ass other half.

"I think it's time I step down from the business. I have so much shit on my mind, and I need to get myself together. I've been doing this street shit for so long that I know it's time. I feel fucked up leaving you because I've been by your side from day one, but if I can't have my mind all in, I won't be in at all. That shit will cause more harm than good." He looked over at me, but I understood him completely. I would never hold him in something he didn't want to be in anymore.

"I love you, man. If this is what you want to do, then I'm not stopping you. You're a very wealthy man. Find something that makes you happy and go live life. It's crazy that you say that because I was thinking about stepping down for the last couple of months and passing this shit off to you and Nori."

Shock covered Malik's face as he drew his head back.

"Are you serious? I mean, I definitely think it's time for you to sit back and enjoy the fruits of your labor," he revealed.

"Yeah, I have to get some things in place, but it's definitely time." I had been contemplating this for a while. After everything that transpired, how my wife was feeling, and the fact that somebody got next to my son changed everything for me. I got a beep on my burner line. I knew it was a text message from Nori. It was a picture of Tasha with a bullet in the center of her forehead. That was another thing that was fucking him up. I did pressure him on that because ultimately, that was a decision he had to make. I slid the phone over to Malik.

"Damn, he did that shit." He sighed.

"I think he's ready to take this organization on his back. He's proven himself time and time again," I announced.

"Yeah, he's definitely ready," he agreed, downing his drink.

"Love you, man. I got some shit to handle. Call me if you need me." He dapped me up and left out. When I walked back upstairs to talk to my wife, she was still in the same spot, looking beautiful as ever. I walked over and pulled her out of bed.

"Babe, I'm working!" She whined.

"And I'm trying to slide these ten inches of heaven in your guts and make your ass shake until you scream and cream. So, what's up? You wanna read that boring shit or do you wanna come sit on this big muthafucka?" I placed gentle kisses on the side of her neck, then her lips.

"It's the dick for me." She wrapped her arms around me, sliding her tongue in my mouth, and I had her damn clothes off before she could blink. Sliding my fingers across her clit caused her to let a moan escape her lips.

"I need you!" She cried out. I lifted her up, placed her on the bed, spread her legs apart, and placed kisses down to her wet pussy. I wasted no time sliding my tongue over her clit and sucking the life out of her shit. Eating pussy was a delicacy, and I loved that shit! My wife never stood a chance when my tongue was wrapped around that pussy. She was losing it, and I enjoyed watching her. If I didn't know shit else, I knew how to please my wife. This dick game was lethal. I could feel her body start to shake, and I knew she was about to bust.

"Let that shit go! Fuck! This pussy wet as fuck. You know I'ma tear this shit up, so don't start your shit!" I growled. The moment she cried out, I replaced my tongue and gave her this dick, inch by fuckin' inch. This shit was so good, and as soon as her pussy muscle tightened around my dick. I tore her ass up. She was trying her best to hold on, but my baby couldn't even form words. "Breathe!" I growled in her ear as I spread her ass cheeks apart and gave her that work.

"Fuck me, baby! Oh God! I'm cumming, baby! She screamed out, locking her pussy down on my dick and that was it for me. We both started cumming. Once we got ourselves together, I pulled her out of bed, and we headed into the bathroom to clean up.

"After your case, I think it's time to take that trip to Bali that you wanted to take. Can you take a month off?" I smiled over at her.

"What! A month? I can do that, but I'm not so sure about you, and where is this coming from?" She questioned, looking so damn sexy and confused.

"I can do whatever I want. After I turn the reigns over to Nori and get him straight, I'm out. You are everything to me, baby. I never want you to feel like I'm not here to care for you and protect you. I want to be here for every part of my son's life." I pulled her in for a kiss.

"Oh my God! You know how much I love you. I can't believe you're doing this. You mean the world to me, and thank you for putting us first. But Lynx, I want you happy as well. Are you sure this is what you want to do?" She asked.

I've been thinking about it for a while, and my brother just helped me out a little more with my decision.

"I'm sure."

It was time for us to step out of the way and retire. Nori got it from here. He's a younger me, and I know that nigga is going to be a force. My life is complete. I made it out the game alive, free, rich, and happily married.

"Babe, what do you think we're going to have this time, a girl or boy?" I snapped my head in her direction so damn fast.

"What! You're pregnant?" I asked, pulling her close.

"We have to go to the doctors, but I took a pregnancy test while you were downstairs, and that's what it says." She laughed. This was life!

My baby is giving me another baby! I couldn't ask for anything more than that. Life is good and I'm happy!

CHAPTER 19
Malik

Driving to my brother's house had me on edge. I knew we had been in this game a long time, and ever since we were young, all we talked about was being the biggest fucking drug lords the world had ever seen. We did that shit too. The thing with dreaming with a young mind is that you don't realize when your dreams become a reality that so much shit will follow with that success. I wasn't the same man. I'd evolved into a person that I barely knew, and while that was scary, it made me feel at peace. This game wasn't for me anymore, and I had to let my brother know that shit.

After telling him how I felt, I was relieved he understood where I was coming from. I have been in the game a long ass time, and I'm tired. I wanted something different for my life. The shit that Mel did to us rocked the fuck out of me and talking with Nori it's taken a toll on him. I knew how much he loved that dirty nigga.

Now that we know Natalie wasn't the mother of that little girl, but Mel was the dad, he was feeling bad about leaving her out there in the world alone. I get where he's coming from, but I'm sure her actual mom has family. Nori was contemplating taking the child in, being that she's his niece.

While I'm sure in a perfect world, that would be the right thing to do, I didn't think it was the smartest. Nori lived just as wild and crazy as we did, but being a father to a child wasn't going to fit in his schedule. Hell, I don't even think Nori is in the mind frame for that shit. That whole thing with Mel, Nat, and ole girl was twisted as fuck, but I guess Mel was fucking them both, and they asses was cool with it.

Another thing that has been weighing down on me is my relationship. I found love, but that shit wasn't as easy as the movies made it. When I stumbled upon Bri, all the red flags were there because baby girl had been through some shit, but being that I was the leader of the Red Flag Boys, I fell for baby girl, and healed her from her past. I became so fucking smitten with her that it was sickening.

I'm 38 years old, it's time to settle down, and I'm hoping that shit can be with Bri. We have been at odds for months, but I refuse to give in to just part of her. For three, almost four years now, I've just had part of her. I knew she didn't mean for me to hear how she felt when she was venting to Sis, but honestly, I knew that shit. When our baby died, Bri changed. She didn't look the same even though she was still fine as fuck. She didn't talk the same, walk the same, or fuck the same. Everything was so robotic with her to the point sometimes I wanted to ask her if she was reading from a script around a nigga. But, for love, I ignored all the new red flags. I deserve all of her. I deserve the same love I give out in return. I would move mountains for that woman.

So, here I was, pulling back up at the home we shared, ready to do what the fuck ever I needed to do to get her back in the right headspace. If she wanted another baby, she could get that after we got some help, and she was rocking my last name. I was willing to do whatever because I felt like I was suffocating without her. My days were long, my nights were short, and my world was in disarray without my baby by my side.

When I walked into our bedroom, shit looked different. The air in the space felt different. Things that normally sat on her dresser were gone. I saw something on the dresser and walked over to see that it was a letter and her ring. My heart began to beat erratically at what I felt this letter said. My mind fluttered with anxiety and frustration as I opened the letter to read it.

Malik, I know when you read this letter, you're going to be angry and probably never want to speak to me again. I hope you understand why I had to do it this way. Truth is, I couldn't look at you. I didn't want to see the hurt in your eyes because I know you've tried to help me heal. I know you have tried to love me through my pain. You may not understand this or me at all. Losing her took a part of me with her, and I lost myself along the way. I'm so sorry for hurting you, that's something I never intended to do.

I thought we would be living life married, with our daughter, and working on another baby, but life doesn't always work the way you want it to. I've prayed so much and talked to God about all of this, and the only thing I could take from our talks is to allow you to live and not have to live through my pain with me. I hope that one day we can come together and have a healthy conversation about this. I just don't think now is the time to do so. I have a lot of healing to do, just know that I will always love you!

Bria

"I can't believe this bitch!" I roared. Tears blurred my vision as I swiped everything from the dresser, with bottles of cologne shattering the floor. She was a fuckin' coward. That's why the fuck she couldn't look me in my fuckin' face! Alarm and anger rippled along my spine. I was so fuckin' mad I couldn't control my emotions, so I proceeded to fucking this room up. I had half a mind to track her fucking phone and send that weak bitch to the same place Natalie, Mel and all the other muthafuckas that wronged us were. I gave this woman everything I had in me, and this is how she treats me! On God, she better stay the fuck away from me!

I picked up my phone to call my brother. When he answered, I went to our text thread and sent the pic of the letter for him to read. I couldn't read that shit again. It would have had me really pulling down on Bri, real talk.

The tears wouldn't stop falling, and I didn't care at this point. It's been a long time since my brother heard me cry, but he was all I had in this moment. Seeing Bri pull this shit had me praying to God that I would never experience no heartbreak like this ever again. This shit hurt worse than getting fucking shot! On Jesus.

"Damn! I'm sorry, bro! I'm so fuckin' sorry!" My brother sighed.

I tried to be strong, but I couldn't help it. I just broke down. I cried for the hurt I was feeling, I cried for the daughter I lost, and I cried for the woman who I thought loved me, but, in the end, I had also lost.

Lynx didn't say much.

Before I knew, it he was walking through the door, wrapping his arms around me in a brotherly hug, and letting me get this shit out.

"It's going to always be us, and you know I got you 'til the muthafuckin' casket drop. I think we have to let Bri go find herself again. She's in a bad place, and even with all that you've tried to do for her, you still couldn't help her.

We as men don't really know how she feels, because we

didn't go through carrying the baby. I know you went through your loss, and you did that shit on your own. I was there for you, but it wasn't like having the woman you lost the baby with being there for you.

Just know when it's time, the one that's meant for you will show up, and she's going to love you like no other woman could. I love you, bro, and you're going to be alright. If you want to come over so that Malayah can love on you, those are her words, by the way, come on over. I found out about this because Bria called Malayah. She wanted me to be with you."

Lifting my head, I swiped my forearm across my swollen eyes and vowed to myself I would never cry over a bitch again.

"Man, on God, FUCK HER!! After I let this go, I'm good. As a matter of fact, I'm back in the game. You said you wanted me and Nori to run shit? I'm all in! Fuck it!"

Made in the USA
Monee, IL
03 October 2023

43894598R00109